A Hard Les[son]

Just then, Slocum sensed [something behind him]
and he wheeled around—[to come] nose to nose with Wash
Trumble.

"Heard somebody was lookin' for me," he growled. "Heard
that somebody was you."

He didn't have his gun drawn. His hands were empty.
And he was staring Slocum right in the eye.

"Guess you heard right," Slocum said softly, his hand
moving, millimeter by millimeter, toward his own holster.

But suddenly, Wash's attention strayed to the kid standing behind Slocum. "Teddy!" Wash roared, and quickly skirted
Slocum to grab Teddy by the shoulders. "I wondered what
become of you, you li'l ol' scamp!"

"Get your hands off'a me," said a scowling Teddy. "Now!"

Surprised, Wash backed off a foot or two, by which time
Slocum had his pistol ready. He buffaloed Wash—banged
him over the head with the butt of his gun—and Wash
dropped to the floor in a heap.

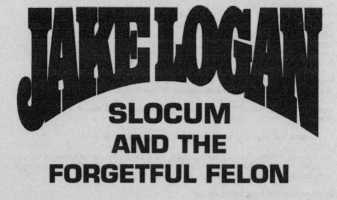

JAKE LOGAN

SLOCUM
AND THE
FORGETFUL FELON

JOVE BOOKS, NEW YORK

THE BERKLEY PUBLISHING GROUP
Published by the Penguin Group
Penguin Group (USA) Inc.
375 Hudson Street, New York, New York 10014, USA

Penguin Group (Canada), 90 Eglinton Avenue East, Suite 700, Toronto, Ontario M4P 2Y3, Canada
(a division of Pearson Penguin Canada Inc.)
Penguin Books Ltd., 80 Strand, London WC2R 0RL, England
Penguin Group Ireland, 25 St. Stephen's Green, Dublin 2, Ireland (a division of Penguin Books Ltd.)
Penguin Group (Australia), 250 Camberwell Road, Camberwell, Victoria 3124, Australia
(a division of Pearson Australia Group Pty. Ltd.)
Penguin Books India Pvt. Ltd., 11 Community Centre, Panchsheel Park, New Delhi—110 017, India
Penguin Group (NZ), 67 Apollo Drive, Rosedale, North Shore 0632, New Zealand
(a division of Pearson New Zealand Ltd.)
Penguin Books (South Africa) (Pty.) Ltd., 24 Sturdee Avenue, Rosebank, Johannesburg 2196,
South Africa

Penguin Books Ltd., Registered Offices: 80 Strand, London WC2R 0RL, England

This is a work of fiction. Names, characters, places, and incidents either are the product of the author's imagination or are used fictitiously, and any resemblance to actual persons, living or dead, business establishments, events, or locales is entirely coincidental.

SLOCUM AND THE FORGETFUL FELON

A Jove Book / published by arrangement with the author

PRINTING HISTORY
Jove edition / November 2010

ISBN: 978-0-515-14858-9

JOVE®
Jove Books are published by The Berkley Publishing Group,
a division of Penguin Group (USA) Inc.
375 Hudson Street, New York, New York 10014.
JOVE® is a registered trademark of Penguin Group (USA) Inc.
The "J" design is a trademark of Penguin Group (USA) Inc.

PRINTED IN THE UNITED STATES OF AMERICA

10 9 8 7 6 5 4 3 2 1

1

In the spring, Slocum found himself down along the border country, riding a chestnut Appaloosa gelding named Ace, and leading a plain bay mare, upon which rode a bound and gagged Teddy Cutler.

Teddy was a young fellow of only twenty-four, but he'd managed to get himself in a pile of trouble far beyond his years. Slocum was leading him toward Bisbee, Arizona Territory, where he planned to turn him in for the reward— $7000, which was a nice-sized chunk of change for somebody like Teddy.

Teddy, who rode with a gag tied around his mouth—the only way Slocum could get any peace—had managed, in his short lifetime, to kill three men, one of which happened to be a U.S. marshal, and stick up four stages. It would have been five, but Teddy'd had the bad luck to try and stick up the stage Slocum was riding on.

That was before Slocum had bought Ace. His old horse, Yucatan, had been shot from beneath him while he was rounding up the Ames boys, up around Denver. He hoped they all hanged. He pretty much counted on their final destination being hell.

Young Teddy Cutler wasn't near so deadly (or deranged) as the Ames boys had been. If he had been, he'd be going into the sheriff's office dead. Slocum'd be skinned if he'd lose another horse to some stick-up artist.

Teddy's gag-muffled mutters of "Mm, mmm mmm *mmm!*" distracted Slocum from his musings. He looked back. Teddy seemed in obvious distress.

"You gotta go?" Slocum asked.

Teddy bobbed his head up and down frantically.

"All right," Slocum said grudgingly, halted Ace, and swung down off him. He went back to Teddy, got his hands unhooked from the saddlehorn, and hauled him down off his mare. "Get it all outta your system," he said as he shoved Teddy toward the weeds. "I wanna get into Bisbee tonight." Three days on the trail, riding like this, was more than enough for Slocum.

It appeared to be enough for Teddy, too. Slocum could hear his urine spatting against the brush from over by the horses. He'd bet Teddy'd be glad to get into a nice cell with a nice chamber pot at hand and nice home-cooked meals— and a mattress that wasn't made up of rocks—just for a change of pace.

He'd hang. That was a given. You couldn't go around shooting U.S. marshals and expect anything else. But in the meantime, Slocum figured Teddy'd appreciate the change in accommodations, if nothing else.

Slocum, himself, was looking forward to a decent hotel bed and the company of one of Miss Lulu's gals. Not necessarily in that order.

The noise from the brush changed. Teddy stumbled back

out on the trail—such as it was—still struggling to finish buttoning his pants with his hands bound.

"Wanta hand?" Slocum asked, even though buttoning another man's breeches wasn't exactly what he wanted to do.

But Teddy shook his head, and finished up himself. Slocum was about to gesture him toward his horse when Teddy tried to say something.

"What?" Slocum asked at the mumble.

Teddy pointed both thumbs toward his gag and said, "Mm mmm!"

"You want the gag off?"

Teddy nodded. "Mm mmm!"

Slocum could understand why he wanted the gag off, but he thought it over for a few minutes, then asked, "Can you keep your mouth shut if I do? No jabberin'?"

Teddy nodded enthusiastically, then turned around so that Slocum could get access to the knot in the bandanna. Slocum slipped it free in a flash, and Teddy sighed, then caught it in his bound hands. "Thanks," he said, then turned back around to face Slocum. The corners of his mouth were red where the gag had chapped them.

It was almost enough to make Slocum feel bad about wanting to have a little peace and quiet on the trail. Almost, but not quite. Teddy could be a regular chatterbox when he put his mind to it.

"C'mon," Slocum said, and motioned toward Teddy's bay. Teddy sighed again, but said nothing, just came and stood at the horse's side and waited. Slocum gave him a boost, retied his hands down to the saddlehorn, picked up his horse's lead rope, and walked forward to remount Ace. He turned his head. "Ready?"

"I reckon," came the reply. It had all the verve and life of a man who knew he was going to hang.

* * *

Slocum and his prisoner arrived in Bisbee right at sunset and Slocum found the sheriff's office with no trouble.

As he helped Teddy down from his horse, he said, "I'm right sorry, Teddy. You're an affable enough feller."

"Not as sorry as I am," Teddy muttered as he hit the ground. Then he turned to his horse's head and took hold of it the best he could, saying, "Hope somebody nice gets you, baby." He kissed her muzzle.

Slocum's hand clasped his upper arm. "I'll see she gets settled at the livery and grained."

"Thanks."

Slocum led him up the steps to the boardwalk and the sheriff's office, then opened the door. The lanterns were lit, and the sheriff was behind the desk with his feet up on it, dozing. When Slocum shut the door behind him, though, the noise woke the sheriff, who came back to lucidity in a big hurry.

He looked up, squinting. "Can I help you fellers?" he asked, his voice still thick with sleep.

"Put on your peepers, Sam," Slocum said. "It's me. Got a prisoner for you."

"What?" asked the sheriff, feeling for his glasses. When he finally found them, buried in a stack of papers, he put them on and looked again. He broke out in grin. "Well, I'll be dogged! How the hell are you, Slocum? And Teddy Cutler, too, if I ain't mistook." He took in the boy's bound hands. "Guess I don't have to ask how you are." He stood, chuckling, and exited his desk. Grabbing a ring of keys off a nail in the wall, he said, "Come with me, fellers."

He led them through a bar-closed door to what he called the "cell block," and opened the last cell on the left, next to a dozing drunk sprawled over his cot. He said, "Do we need these now, Slocum?" and pointed to the ropes that bound Teddy's wrists.

Slocum said, "Nope, you can get rid of 'em anytime. And we had a long ride. He might could do with a cup of coffee and some supper." He felt himself beginning to feel sorry for young Teddy, but told himself that there was a dead U.S. marshal out there with Teddy's bullet in his back, and the regret went away fast. Mostly.

Sheriff Sam—whose last name Slocum could never remember except that it had a lot of C's and Z's and Y's in it—pulled the final knot free at last and closed the cell door. "Guess that'll do it for now," he said. "Coffee or water?" he asked Teddy.

"Coffee," came the subdued reply.

Sam exited the cell block and was back with a steaming mug before Slocum got all the way to the main cell door. He was slowed by those thoughts again, thoughts he pushed down as fast as they arose. Trouble was, they just kept pushing back up again.

Slocum and Sheriff Sam stopped by the saloon after Slocum got the horses put up. The crowd was thin, and Slocum asked Sam where everybody was. When he'd been in before, there had always been a goodly crowd, even on a weeknight. But tonight, there were less than a dozen men in the place, including the bartender.

"Copper's dryin' up," Sam said matter-of-factly as they bellied up to the bar.

"This much?"

Sam nodded. "They're layin' off miners hand over fist. Don't know where most of 'em are goin', 'cept maybe up to Colorado. We lost about thirty percent of the town in just the last month or so."

Slocum shook his head. "It's a cryin' shame, ain't it. I hear Tombstone ain't doin' so well either."

"You heard right," Sam answered. "Ever since the Earps pulled out, the town ain't been the same. And on top of that, they got flooding mines."

"That's what I heard," Slocum said, just as the bartender appeared. "Beer," he said to the bartender. "Where's Roy?"

The bartender said, "Same for you, Sam?" When Sam nodded, he turned back to Slocum. "Roy, he up and took his wife and boys back to Texas after he got canned. Business just ain't what it was. Old Man Nobby only hired me 'cause I'd work for a room to live in and fifteen bucks a month. He fired the gals, too, so there was plenty'a rooms to pick from." Slowly, he shook his head. "Helluva thing." He moved off toward the beer kegs.

Slocum shook his head. "Helluva thing is right."

After spending a too-quiet night at the hotel and arranging for Sam to wire the reward money to his account in the Tombstone bank, Slocum groomed Ace's hide up to a fairly glittering copper shine, and set out the next morning, heading north. If he was lucky, he thought, he could make Tombstone by nightfall. Maybe there'd be *somebody* around who remembered him.

But when he got there, there wasn't.

He didn't spy a blasted soul he recognized. The Earps were gone, having pulled up stakes and headed for California, and even Doc Holliday had disappeared along with his longtime gal, Big Nose Kate. Slocum was beginning to think he was all alone in the world. Hell, he couldn't even dig up any familiar female companionship, and he had to put his own horse up at the livery!

He knew he'd been away for a coon's age, but this was ridiculous.

When he went by the bank, it was closed, of course, so he thought he'd best come back in the morning. He figured that his money would be safer—all of it—in a bank up in Phoenix. After he took a short walking tour of the town, visiting places that weren't even places anymore and trying to dig himself up a gal, he finally gave up and went to bed alone with a bottle of halfway decent bourbon and a cheap cigar.

It was better than nothing.

2

Slocum woke early, with thoughts of Teddy Cutler thudding and thrashing around in his brain like a dying steer in the butcher's shed. It was the last thing he needed. But even after he dressed, went for breakfast, went to the bank, and walked out again—after arranging to transfer his money to the bank in Phoenix and withdrawing $200 for pocket cash—he still stood on the boardwalk, pocketing the bills, and thinking about the kid.

It wasn't really fair, was it? Sure, the kid had killed more than his share and had the misfortune of including a U.S. marshal in the mix, but after spending a few days leading him east across hard country, Slocum was convinced Teddy'd changed. For the better, of course.

He shook his head. There was nothing more he could do about it. If he hadn't picked up Teddy, somebody else would have. And they likely wouldn't have asked him any questions either—just shot him and hauled his carcass in for the cash.

Slocum started up toward the livery, his long legs making short work of the distance. Well, he thought as he entered the barn, Teddy was nothing if not charming. Mayhap he could talk his way out of it. Slocum silently wished him all the luck in the world, and began tacking up his horse for the long ride to Phoenix.

Three days later at about eleven in the morning, Slocum rode into Phoenix. First thing, he went to the bank and found they had received Tombstone's wire about the money, and that his cash would be available to him on the morrow. He said his thanks, then made his way to the livery, where he paid extra to a redheaded kid to have Ace put up right and grained twice daily.

It had been several years since he'd been through town, and he found it had grown by leaps and spurts, and showed no signs of stopping anytime soon. He supposed it had the right. This year, the territorial capital had been moved down here from Prescott—again—and the whole city had taken on a new sheen. Buildings were going up every which way in town, and the residential area he'd ridden through on his way in was spreading out its tentacles, too.

Miss Kate's place was still right where he'd left it, though, and he'd no more than set a foot over her threshold when he was bombarded with unexpected squeals and cries of glee and what, at first, appeared to be a million pair of hands, all reaching to hug him. He recovered quickly, though, backed up, and raised his hand to cover his face while, miraculously, avoiding stepping on any female feet or toes.

"Whoa!" he shouted over their clamor. "Give a feller a break, ladies!"

Slowly, the gabfest died down and Slocum was able to tell the girls apart. Some he knew, some he didn't, but there was one he knew very well indeed. Standing back, apart from the crowd, was the house's redheaded madam, and with a chuckle behind her eyes, she was staring straight at him.

He said, "Hello, Kate."

And she said, "About time, Slocum."

He let out a soft chuckle. "Aw, Katie. You missed me. I'm touched."

Slowly, her arms wrapped around her waist, she moved forward. "You better be. And you wanna know how much," she said, "c'mon upstairs and I'll show you."

A murmur, punctuated by giggles, broke out in the crowd of girls as, about a foot away from Slocum, she came to a stop. He looked down at her. She'd made no attempt to touch him yet—hadn't thrown her arms around him, hadn't even ventured to put forth a finger—but behind those green eyes there glowed a fire that he knew could never, would never, be put out.

He didn't speak. He couldn't. A hot thickness had suddenly risen in his throat and behind his eyes, and rather than open his mouth and look like a fool, he merely took her elbow in his hand and started toward the stairs.

Behind them, the girls let out a sweet, soft sigh, en masse.

Brother! he thought. *Am I gettin' soft or what?*

He had to chuckle to himself on the way up the stairs, though. He wasn't going soft. In fact, he didn't believe he'd ever been so hard—and so far away from a bed—in his life.

"Somethin' strike you funny, Slocum?" Katie asked as they gained the top of the stairs and started down the hall toward her room. They couldn't get there fast enough to suit him.

"Nothin' to speak of. At the moment anyhow," he said.

She put her hand on the latch and opened the door. "Here we are."

"Not soon enough to suit me!" he said, and sweeping

her up in his arms, he carried her inside, kicked the door closed behind him, and deposited her on the bed.

Her eyes traveled down his front—and stopped at his crotch. She smiled a little. "I can see why, you big ol' eager beaver, you." She began to unbutton her skirt.

"Hurry," he said. He was already out of his shirt and pants and boots, and was ripping at the buttons of his long johns.

She barely had a path cleared for him in time. All he knew was that he was inside her, and he was working it for all it was worth. He must have been really engorged, because she gasped when he entered her, and was still wide-eyed as, pounding away, he kissed her neck, then dropped his head to nuzzle at her breasts.

The nuzzling didn't last long, though. He felt a strong rumbling deep down in his belly—familiar, powerful, and overwhelming—that swiftly traveled lower and lower until—

"Argh . . ." he groaned, and collapsed, flat out, on Katie.

He lay there for almost a minute, panting with the sheer relief of it, the sheer bliss, when Katie said softly, "I take it you're done?"

Despite himself, a deep chuckle rose up his throat, and without moving, he replied, "Hang on a second, honey. I was as wound up a nickel-plated watch. Couldn't hold it back."

"What's got you so stirred up?"

"Not sure, except I ain't had any since Saturday week."

There was a grin in Katie's voice. "Surprised you didn't explode. No, wait. You did."

Slocum chortled softly. And he felt himself rising to the occasion already!

Katie's arms went around his neck. She said, "Feels like you're gearin' up for some more action, Slocum. Feels like you're gearin' up in a hurry, too!"

He was, and he began again, this time slower, this time with his old, steady control back in place. He worked himself like a practiced swordsman; thrusting, parrying, but always coming back to the center, always burying himself deep in her hot and pulsing core, until Katie spasmed and cried out his name. That put him over the edge, too.

They clung to each other for a good long time.

They didn't come down until the next morning, both with smiles on their sleepy-eyed faces, and the girls hanging around in the kitchen covered their mouths, trying to hide their giggles. They didn't succeed, though.

"All right," Slocum said to the group. "Just get it out of your systems."

Hands went to their sides and a few giggles escaped, but mostly, the girls were all smiles and grins.

"All right, then," Katie announced. "Off with you. Shoo!"

Slowly, the girls filed out, until Slocum and Katie were left alone in the kitchen. "Finally," Katie said, and only then did she break out in a smile. "I s'pose they wanted to make certain I lived through it," she said. "Been a long spell since I went upstairs with a man."

Slocum, who had pulled out a chair and sat himself down at the table, perked up at that. "Who? When?" Then he caught himself. "Sorry, Kate. None'a my business."

She had begun to serve them some breakfast, and as she spooned scrambled eggs onto two plates, she said, "Oh, it's your business, all right. It's been goin' on four years, and it was you."

She slid a plate in front of Slocum—eggs, bacon, hash browns, and toast—and added, "You remember?"

He did. He was trackin' a feller and stopped through town. He also remembered that he'd taken on a stray little gal, right here at Katie's, and delivered her to her family out in California.

He spoke. "I remember. That was sure a doozy of a deal

you got me into that time." He spoke with a smile on his lips, to let her know there were no hard feelings, because there weren't. He was a big boy. He could get himself in—and out—of trouble all on his own.

He changed the subject. "Town's sure different."

"Phoenix, you mean?"

"Yup."

"You're not just whistlin' Dixie. Got all kinds of new things goin' up, and old ones comin' down." She sat beside him and joined him in breakfast. "Hope they decide to keep the capital here for good this time. Hate to see them stop puttin' up all them pretty new buildings." She munched on a strip of bacon. "Tess is gettin' to be a pretty good cook, don't'cha think?"

"Not as good as you, Katie, but pretty damn decent." A huge bite of toast spread with cactus jelly prevented him from further discourse.

That didn't stop Katie, though. "How long you stayin' this time, Slocum?"

He swallowed, then smiled at her. "Got no particular plans at the moment. Reckon I'll stay 'til you get sick'a me and send me packin'."

She laughed, and swatted him on the arm. "As if I'd ever do that!"

And she didn't either. Slocum stayed over for about a week, while he waited for his voucher to clear. He wanted to leave, but something—besides Katie's nightly ministrations, that was—kept him rooted in place.

"Slocum, I swan! You're as jumpy as a bag full'a bobcats!" she said to him one evening.

He turned toward her. He'd been pacing her bedroom floor in his long johns, a cigar in one hand and an empty bourbon tumbler in the other.

"I can't help it, Katie." He shrugged his shoulders. "I just feel like something's gonna happen. Hell, I dunno. Something's in the wind, though." He took the last drag on his cigar, then stubbed it out in a crystal ashtray. Katie had real pretty things.

A furrow appeared in her forehead. "What d'you mean by 'something'? A sandstorm? Indians? Outlaws? Jesus gonna come down and snatch us all up to a higher plane? What?"

He snorted out a little laugh. "Nothin' so dramatic, Katie. Just . . . something . . ." He stopped to stare out the window. He'd be damned if he knew what it was.

He wished like hell that he did, so that he could ignore it and just ride out of town. But he couldn't ignore it, and not knowing what it was that he couldn't ignore was driving him crazy.

"Well, starin' out the window in your underwear ain't gonna get you anyplace," Katie said after a few minutes. The night had gone chilly, and she pulled the sheet more tightly about her shoulders. "Come back to bed, baby. Keep me warm."

He looked at her, then grinned. "You asked for it, Katie. Remember that."

"Oh, I won't forget," she answered, laughing. "You can just bet I won't!"

He hit the bed so hard that the breeze from his landing blew out the candle on his bed stand. The only thing left to illuminate the room was the feeling he got when Katie took him in her hands. He stiffened immediately.

She said, "That's my big ol' boy. Now, c'mon and do what you do best." She began to move her hands on him.

Well, there were just some women—and some acts— you couldn't say "no" to.

He didn't.

3

The next morning, he found out just what the wind had dredged up.

He took a walk over to the U.S. marshal's office, and was met by Pete Stanford, the big chief himself. Pete—a tall, slender, sandy-haired man of middle age—ushered him into his office, sat himself and Slocum on opposite sides of his wide walnut desk, and making short work of it, said, "Teddy Cutler escaped. Need the cash back."

Slocum scowled. Seven grand, down the drain. He said, "How?"

"Sheriff down to Bisbee said he was there when he went to dinner, and gone when he came back. That's all there is to it. Sheriff said it was like he pulled off the best magic trick ever." He shrugged.

"Anybody see him?"

Pete shook his head. "Not on the street, not at the stable, not a single soul has spoke up to date. The whole town's deaf and dumb. I take it he was a likable feller?"

Slocum nodded in the affirmative.

"Sometimes those are the toughest to deal with." He paused, sighing. "Right sorry about the money, Slocum."

"Me, too."

"I'll bet."

Slocum left the marshal's office with mixed feelings. Sure, he was mad about the money, but he couldn't help giving a silent cheer for Teddy. In the end, he just silently walked up to the bank and arranged to have the $7000 put back in the marshal's business account.

Now, he wasn't poor. Over the years, he'd managed to put over twenty-some thousand in his Tombstone account— now his Phoenix account—and roughly the same amount in accounts throughout the Western states and territories. Money had never meant that much to him. It just sort of landed in his lap from riding the range and getting himself into, well, situations. Usually with folks who needed jobs done, or men with paper out on them.

None of it was money he'd stolen. He'd given that up long ago. No, he was strictly on the legalities these days, even though, in a few backwoods localities, there was still paper on him. He supposed he could buy himself a real mansion if he wanted to, get himself a butler and maid to boot. But that'd mean settling down, and his feet still itched too much for him to do that.

He was most of the way to the nearest saloon when he walked right into somebody, somebody with his back turned toward him. The man turned to face him while he was still reeling from the impact and opened his mouth, but no sound came out.

Slocum'd be damned if he didn't know that face.

"Teddy Cutler," he said, trying to decide in a slap second whether to pound him on the back in congratulations or to skin him alive right there on the spot.

Teddy smiled wide, a smile that went clear up to his light blue eyes. "Sky eyes," Slocum's ma had always called them. He grew up with a kid who was nicknamed Sky because of them.

"Howdy, Slocum," Teddy said, still grinning. "Been at least a week, week and a half, ain't it?"

"Round about." Slocum was still thinking about the pounding on the back or the skinning. "You were in a whole different circumstance when I last saw you."

"That I was, that I was. Oh, I near forgot!" he said, stepping to the side to expose a pretty young lady in a pale green dress. "Want to introduce you to Miss Alice Swan. Alice, meet John Slocum."

She curtsied, and Slocum kissed her gloved hand, in the Southern manner. He hadn't been raised in a barn. He said, "Charmed, Miss Swan."

"Honored, Mister Slocum, sir," she replied.

"It's just Slocum, if you please, miss." She was certainly pretty enough, but he was having trouble reading just what was going on behind those warm brown eyes.

She curtsied again, just halfway, and smiled. "As you wish, Slocum." She turned toward Teddy. "Your friends are as polite as you are, sir."

Teddy was lapping it up, every syllable, every nuance. Not Slocum. He still couldn't figure her game, but if she "sirred" him one more time . . .

"We was just goin' for a bite to eat, Slocum. Care to join us?" Teddy was smitten, sure as shooting. By the looks of it, he was too busy thinking about Miss Alice Swan to consider that Slocum had every right to slug him upside the head and haul him on down to the marshal's office.

Slocum was considering it, though.

Instead of answering Teddy's invitation, Slocum said, "How'd you do it, Teddy? How'd you get out?"

Teddy turned a curious eye on him. "How'd I get out of what? C'mon, Slocum, let's go get some lunch!"

Either Teddy had blanked out his incarceration, or he was the best straight-faced liar Slocum had ever met. But he decided to give the kid the benefit of the doubt. For now anyway.

"Let's eat," he said to Teddy, and the three of them set off for Joe's Café.

Slocum was halfway through with his beef sandwich and beer when the marshal and one of his deputies walked into the café, and made straight for his table.

He barely had time to hiss "Teddy" before the deputy was standing behind the boy's chair, a cocked pistol at his neck.

Teddy, a look of bewilderment on his face, gulped hard and said, "If you fellers are stickin' me up, you'd be diggin' a dry well. I got only enough money on me to pay for my lunch!"

Standing to one side, the marshal slowly shook his head, then looked over at Slocum. "Should I haul you in, too?"

"Nope," Slocum said. "Was trying to make up my mind about takin' him into custody. Just ran into them, outside on the walk."

The marshal nodded, then narrowed his gaze. "Tryin' to make up your mind?"

Slocum tipped his head to the right, toward Miss Alice Swan. "I kinda thought he was already in custody. Bounty hunter."

Alice ripped her napkin from her lap and threw it on the table. "I certainly am *not* a bounty hunter. I am a self-employed, self-motivated finder of lost persons."

"Who just happen to carry a bounty on their heads."

She sniffed at him. "Slocum, you are most annoying."

Marshal Pete waved his arms. "Whoa, whoa, whoa! Just hold up, you two." To the deputy, he said, "Dave, let's get Teddy here into the lockup. Slocum, you and the lady come along so's I can get this thing at least halfway straight in my head."

Forty-five minutes later, Marshal Pete was still shaking his sandy-haired head in befuddlement. And Slocum was getting tired of trying to explain something that he, himself, didn't understand. Finally, Miss Swan, who had so far remained silent on a corner bench, spoke up.

"It's called amnesia, gentlemen," she said as she stood up. "Either he was struck just so on the head, or he experienced something extremely traumatic. Traumatic enough to make him switch over to this new version of Teddy."

Marshal Pete narrowed his eyes. "What you mean, traumatic, Miss Swan?"

Frowning, Slocum echoed, "Speak English, Alice."

She sniffed at both of them. "An experience leading to trauma. Some soldiers came back from the War Between the States traumatized. Some of them are still taking up space in our madhouses and lunatic asylums."

The marshal asked her to go on, but Slocum needed no further explanation. He knew somebody who'd been traumatized by the War—Mr. Wilcox, their nearest neighbor, about four miles down the pike, back home. Something had happened to Mr. Wilcox, his pa had told him. Something bad enough that he came home a changed man. Where he'd always been a fair man, he became niggardly, and three times he showed up at Slocum's parents' place, wanting to "untrade" a horse he'd sold them better than ten years back, and which had since died of old age.

He claimed no knowledge of the War—or *any* war.

It was as if, his father wrote, something had wiped the

slate of Mr. Wilcox's mind clean, excepting the few things that were pleasant to remember: his family and his home, and scattered events in his past.

The last Slocum had heard, Mr. Wilcox was still off his nut after all these years, still wanting his horse back, and still denying that there ever had been a War. He'd likely go to his grave that way, too.

So, Slocum tended to think that Alice was right about Teddy. He didn't much like her, but she was right. And the minute she shut up, he said so.

"You sure, Slocum?" Marshal Pete asked, brows lifted.

"Pretty much. We had a neighbor back home that had the same thing."

"He ever get over it?"

Slocum shook his head. "Nope. Far as I know, he's still denying that he was in the Army, and that he was a major, and that there ever was a War. Thinks everybody else is crazy."

"What about the time he was away?" the marshal asked. "Must'a been years. How'd he account for that?"

"Accordin' to him, he'd been downstate, visitin' his sister. For a week."

Marshal Pete slowly shook his head. "This's a new one on me. If a man kills three people, including a U.S. marshal, but he don't recall doin' it, can it be fair to take him to trial, then hang him?"

Slocum looked down at his boots. He shook his head.

But Miss Swan spoke up loud and clear. "It doesn't matter what we think is fair. He did the killings, and now he must pay for them in a court of law. And I hereby claim the reward."

The marshal looked at her pretty face. "No," he said. "This here's America, and this here's my territory. I make the rules."

Slocum refrained from reminding him that he was only a cog in a very large legal machine.

"And?" demanded Miss Swan.

"I'll give you my decision tomorrow afternoon."

Miss Alice Swan stood abruptly, nearly knocking the bench over in the process. Saying, "Tomorrow, then," she let herself out. The door slammed behind her.

"Thanks, Pete," Slocum said after a moment. "For givin' him the benefit of the doubt, I mean." He thumbed back his hat. "Sure wish I knew what brought this on."

The marshal nodded and muttered something about wishes and horses that Slocum didn't understand, and then he stood up. Slocum followed suit.

"You put the money back?" Pete asked.

"Into your business account."

"Right. See you tomorrow. And by the way, *if* we decide to keep him and go to trial, half that reward's yours."

Slocum grunted. "Don't make me feel no better."

"I know how you feel, buddy," said Pete, sneering toward the door. "I know how you feel."

By the time Slocum emerged from the marshal's office, Miss Alice Swan was nowhere in sight, so he headed on down toward Katie's place. He was hungry, on top of everything else. He'd had only half a sandwich, after all.

He wondered about Teddy. Had they taken him something, brought it to his cell? And then he had some harsh words with himself. *Don't you go gettin' soft on me,* he thought. *He's a murderer. Don't you forget it.*

He kept walking till he came to the edge of town, the place where the trees started, although they were still sparse. As he turned in at Katie's walk, things seemed more settled. He didn't know why, but they just did. The thought crossed his mind that maybe it was his proximity to Katie's presence, but there were too many thoughts today, too much confusing information.

And Slocum was a man who didn't like to be confused. Not for an instant.

4

While Alice Swan, although troubled, slept in comfort in her hotel room, and Slocum spent his night with the lovely Miss Katie, Teddy Cutler was not so fortunate.

Why wouldn't anybody listen to him? What had he done to land himself in jail like this? And when was somebody going to come and talk some sense into these boys?

He paced and he paced, but he couldn't come up with a decent reason for being here in the first place. All he did was ride his horse into town. And this was beyond him. Hell, they hadn't even bothered to tell him what he was charged with!

Finally, after very nearly wearing a path into the brick floor of his cell, he slouched down on his cot, still confused as ever. He leaned back, twisting until he could get a glimpse of the big clock in the front office. It read twelve thirty-four.

He had a long wait until tomorrow.

Come to think of it, he couldn't even remember when he'd first met Slocum. Good ol' Slocum, for God's sake!

Teddy cursed beneath his breath, then tried to make himself comfortable. But there was no position that brought him any relief whatsoever from the questions that gnawed at him.

The lovely Miss Alice Swan dozed fitfully in her room at the hotel. They wouldn't let Cutler go, they couldn't! First off, they'd spoil her perfect record, and second, it just plain wasn't legal, so far as she could figure.

Teddy Cutler had killed three people, and he had to pay. Period. No matter what sort of mental mishmash he'd come up with to try and wriggle out of it. She was certain of it, certain that they'd all burn in hell if they let him go. Well, with the exception of her, of course. She had been practically on her way to the marshal's office—after tracking Teddy for eight long months—when they were stopped by that blasted Slocum character!

In her sleep, she grimaced. She was a lot tougher than she looked on the outside. And she'd be damned if she'd let anybody—even the famous John Slocum!—steal a bounty out from under her!

The next morning found Slocum in Miss Katie's kitchen, having a cup of coffee while he waited for his eggs and flapjacks. The clock on the wall told him it was a little past ten, but he was in no hurry. Marshal Pete had said he'd make his decision in twenty-four hours, so he figured he had about four hours to fill up before then.

Finally, Kate slid his breakfast plate before him: eggs, pancakes with syrup, crisp bacon, and steaming, crisp hash browns. It was more than he'd expected! "Whoa, Katie!" he exclaimed. "You didn't have to go to so much trouble for me!"

She sat down next to him. "Ain't no trouble," she said, trailing a finger up his arm. "Not when it's for you."

Now Slocum was grateful, but nervous. Katie had been a good match for him all these years, but he wasn't ready to settle down, not by a long shot. And he didn't care for feeling like he was being railroaded into it!

"Now, Katie," he began between bites of her pancakes. "The trail is callin' me already."

She smiled. "Bet you won't answer it till you've finished those flapjacks, at least."

Slocum chuckled. "You've got that right, honey."

She leaned back in her chair and picked up a piece of her bacon, nibbling at it. "You always gonna have itchy feet, Slocum?"

"You askin' if I'm ever gonna settle down?"

"That's it."

"Well," he said, and paused to swallow a bite of eggs. "It depends. If you're askin' me for now, the answer is no, never. Gonna wander till I die. But ask me another time, I might tell you different." He shrugged. "Sorry I can't tell you somethin' more firm."

She leaned in toward the table, and picked up her fork. "Well, I s'pose if you can't, you can't."

Disappointment rang heavy in her voice, but Slocum didn't say anything else. He was afraid he'd just stir up more trouble, and trouble wasn't something he wanted with Katie. Not now, not ever.

"How're things goin' at the marshal's office?" she asked him, abruptly changing the subject. It couldn't have come at a better time.

"So-so," he said. "Pete allowed as how he might just let Teddy go, the circumstances bein' so odd and all, but he didn't make no promises. Not till this afternoon anyhow."

"And you have that woman bounty hunter to deal with, too."

"Yeah," he replied, taking a bite of his eggs. "Whatshername. Alice Somethin'. Don't trust her no farther than I could throw her."

"Why?"

"She's a female bounty hunter, for one thing. And she's just too . . . I dunno. Too something. Like she's practiced to be perfect too much, y'know?"

Katie said, "I think so. She pretty?"

Now, that was a cougar of a question just waiting to bite him in the butt! He stalled a moment by chewing too long, then gulping coffee. "Don't rightly know. I mean, she has blond hair and she was wearing a blue—no, mayhap it was green—dress. Anyhow, blue or green. And she looked and acted, I dunno, Southern, I guess. But outside of that, I couldn't tell you."

Katie wouldn't let go of it. She asked, "Southern, like from South America? Was she Mexican?"

Slocum allowed himself a laugh. "No, more like the American South."

"Oh," said Katie, just as Mary, one of the girls, entered the room all aflutter and asked Katie where something or other was. Katie excused herself, and that was the end of it.

Thank God.

Teddy had thought and thought on it all night, and he still couldn't recall where he and Slocum had first met. Which was odd, because Teddy prided himself on having a first-class memory. Things seemed to be changing, though. Like when that pretty little gal, Miss Alice Swan, approached him yesterday, asking for directions, and he could've sworn on his grandma's grave that he recognized her! He didn't know from where or when, but he knew her, all right, even though she acted like he was a total stranger to her, and all she wanted was directions to "an eating establishment."

He still didn't know why they were making him stay here. They'd had a doctor come to see him this morning, a doctor who asked a lot of questions, most of which didn't make any sense, and didn't once tap his knees with a little hammer or look down his throat. Some crazy kind of doctor, he was.

Mostly, he just talked. And it wasn't medical stuff either. It was mostly questions. Like, how did he know Slocum (a subject he was still pondering on), and how did he get to Phoenix, and where was his horse stabled? And then the questions got even crazier!

Where was he on March seventh? Damned if he knew. Who paid attention to calendars when they were ridin' the trail?

Had he ever carried a Smith & Wesson pistol? He didn't think so. And he was pretty sure he'd recall if he had. The few he'd seen were so long-barreled it'd take a half hour to pull 'em free of your holster.

Had he recently suffered a serious bodily injury? Like, did he hit his head on anything, or had he been struck unconscious? No, he was pretty sure he'd recall somethin' like that. Well, there was a time, when he was about nine or ten, that the neighborhood bully, Big Billy Bester, had knocked him out for a four-hour stretch during recess. When he woke up, school was closed and everybody was gone except for Miss Gates, the schoolmarm, and his mother, who'd been rushed in from their farm.

In case he died, he supposed.

He'd been arrested in the company of the famous bounty hunter, Slocum, the doctor told him. Of course, he already knew about Slocum, but the famous part was new to him. "Famous bounty hunter?" he said, and shook his head. "The things folks don't tell you!"

The doctor cocked one eyebrow. "Slocum didn't tell you he was a bounty hunter?"

Teddy laughed. "He didn't say nothin' about bein' famous neither! Can you beat that?"

After a few more questions, the doctor left Teddy alone. The clock on the outer office wall said it was a few minutes past noon. Which meant it was about an hour till Slocum would show up. Well, maybe they'd break up the time by having his lunch delivered.

He hoped.

Slocum arrived at the marshal's office at one on the dot—and with Miss Alice Swan directly on his heels.

Alice had a smug expression on her pretty little face, and Slocum was considering smacking it off when Marshal Pete opened his door and invited them into his office. Slocum couldn't read his face, but he sure could tell what was on Alice's mind. She practically had both hands out for that reward. Slocum hoped she was wrong, wrong, wrong.

He'd been doing some thinking, too. And he'd decided that anybody deserved a chance to straighten up and fly right.

Especially Teddy.

After all, Teddy had those whatchacall things, those "mitigating circumstances." After yesterday, Slocum wholeheartedly believed this to be true. Seemed it made no difference to Miss Alice Swan, though, because her opening comment, once they got in the office and got sat down opposite Marshal Pete, was, "I assume you have my money ready, Marshal?"

Slocum slouched in his chair, and shook his head, sighing. God, she was a mercenary bitch!

But Pete surprised them both by saying, "No, I'm afraid I don't, Miss Swan. Slocum, Miss Swan, I been up half the night frettin' about this thing, over 'n over again."

Alice growled under her breath while Slocum cocked his head, riveted on Pete's next words.

"Slocum," Pete said, "I'm releasin' him into your custody. We had the doc over, Miss Swan, and he couldn't break his story. He even slipped him some laudanum, and it didn't make no difference. Slocum, I want you to ride with him for six months, and keep your eyes open."

"Six months?" Slocum protested.

"That's what I said. Where you go, he goes. No exceptions. And at the end of six months, you bring him back here to check in. If I'm convinced at that time that he's tellin' the truth and he really don't remember, then I'll get those charges dropped. Otherwise, he's going back into custody until the day he dies. You all right with all that, Slocum?"

Slocum nodded. He guessed he had to be, to save Teddy.

Alice Swan, who had been silent while the terms of Teddy's release were spelled out, suddenly leaned forward and pounded her fist on the desk. "I protest!" she announced.

"Good for you, Miss Swan," Sheriff Pete said, nodding. "Howsoever, it ain't gonna do you no good." Then, with no fanfare, Pete stood up. Slocum followed suit. Miss Swan glowered at them both. Slocum decided he couldn't really blame her, but that disgusted expression wiped all the pretty off her face.

The pretty didn't come back until they had both followed Pete outside, to the main office. Pete signaled to one of the deputies, who rose from his desk and paperwork to go back into the cell block.

He appeared again in short order, dragging Teddy Cutler behind him.

"Quit squirmin'!" the deputy barked. "I already told you, it ain't nothin' bad!" And then, with one huge effort, the deputy hauled back and yanked a reluctant Teddy practically off his feet and to the foreground.

Teddy raised his eyes slowly, then recognized his visitors. His face lit up. "Hello, Miss Swan, Slocum! You finally manage to talk some sense into these folk?"

Neither had a chance to respond, because Pete, grabbing Teddy's arm, said, "Wantcha t'come on back to my office, Teddy. Got a deal to talk over with you. You come too, Slocum. Miss Swan, thank you for comin' by."

He looked toward the deputy, who waited behind Teddy. "Thanks, Harley. Believe you can get back to your paperwork now."

5

Miss Alice Swan watched the marshal and Teddy, followed by Slocum, go into the marshal's office, then close the door behind them. She was fit to be tied over the whole damned affair. Not only had they snatched her bounty away, but they'd broken her ongoing record—well, ongoing until this day, that was—for the most consecutive arrests by a female bounty hunter ever.

She was proud of that record. In some towns, she ate out on it. Not Phoenix, though.

She let herself out, then spat on their sidewalk. Crazy damned rubes! Damned *cheap* crazy rubes! Back home, in Santa Fe, they wouldn't have let this . . . this travesty of justice happen! Good God! Even in *Texas* this wouldn't have happened!

And she ought to know. She was from Texas, born and raised in El Paso. And the law had some bark on it back home!

Grumbling beneath her breath, she stalked back to her

hotel, where she could have some peace and quiet while she thought what to do next.

Pete finished his talk to Teddy, and Teddy was confused, to say the least. He got the part where he was in Slocum's custody—although he couldn't figure why. He got that he was supposed to stay with Slocum for six months, then check in here again, at the marshal's office. And on and on and on.

At last, the marshal finished. "You got all that, Teddy?"

Teddy nodded. "Can I ask a question?"

The marshal nodded. Slocum hadn't said a word since they entered the office.

Teddy looked straight into the marshal's eyes. "Why? What'd I do?"

A pained expression crossed the marshal's face before he said, "Can't say, Teddy."

Teddy twisted toward Slocum. "Will somebody tell me what's goin' on around here? Slocum?"

But the big man did nothing except shrug his shoulders.

Resolutely, Teddy crossed his arms and leaned back in his chair. "This don't make no sense."

But the marshal shook his head. "Makes all the sense in the world, Teddy, iffen you got the whole story. Which you ain't gonna get until six months from now, if I got anything to do with it." He slid a look at Slocum, who nodded, but made a face.

And Teddy thought, *I'm not gonna get an answer out of him either, dammit!* He said, "Will ya tell me then? In six months, I mean."

"Said I would," replied the marshal. "You agree to all the terms an' conditions I just set forth?"

Teddy would have agreed to sell his best friend for crackers—if he could remember having a best friend, that was—to get the heck out of this place. And so he nodded and said, "Yes. I do, sir." And hoped to the saints that he looked credible when he said it.

Apparently he did, because the marshal skidded his chair back and stood up. "Six months, Slocum," he said. "Or a damn good reason. And you stay in the Territory. Can't be responsible for anythin' that happens outside the Arizona borders."

"You oughta pay me for this, Pete," Teddy heard Slocum grumble.

"Plannin' on it," the marshal said, "in a sorta sideways way. Got a whole file of papers for fellers wanted right here in the Territory. Take your druthers."

The marshal opened the door, and Slocum and Teddy, still puzzled, followed him out into the other room, where the marshal asked in a booming voice, "Who's got the file? The current one."

A short fellow two desks away from them held up a hand. "I do," he said, and began searching through a pile of papers. Eventually, he handed it over to the marshal, who in turn handed it to Slocum. "You can take it. I got copies in the files, over there." He nodded toward the wall, where four filing cabinets stood.

Slocum said, "Thanks, Pete," and tucked the file under his arm. "Let's go, Teddy."

Teddy nodded. He was more than ready to leave.

Slocum, with Teddy tagging despondently at his heels, headed straight for Katie's place. He didn't know if the kid had eaten, but he figured that Katie'd have something on the stove besides coffee. She usually did.

He knew the other gals'd be glad for Teddy's company, too, though he wanted to have a word with Teddy before he turned him loose in there. Slocum figured he'd pay for

Teddy for the first two, no, three, times, but after that he was on his own. Those gals were hungry for business, now that the town was rising up.

A person would have thought that it'd be the other way around, but the jump in population had brought a jump in whorehouses, too, which meant that whores were currently a dime a dozen. Business had been slow. Katie had even mentioned retiring. Several times.

At first, he'd thought it was only her "settle down and procreate" impulse. All women had it, he figured. Hell, they wouldn't be women without it. But now he was seeing that it was something deeper.

"Left up here," he said to Teddy.

"Where we goin'?" Teddy asked. "And besides that, where we goin' for six goddamn months!"

"Promised I wouldn't tell you," Slocum said as they took the turn. "Made a solemn pledge."

"To that marshal? Who's he to you anyhow?"

"'That marshal' is U.S. Marshal Pete Stanford, and he's the head lawman for the whole of the Territory," Slocum said as they gained Katie's porch. "He's a good man, and he's got his own good reasons for chuckin' you into my custody. Now, no more questions. And behave yourself."

Slocum opened the front door and ushered Teddy inside. They were met by several of the girls, all of whom were immediately taken with Teddy. And he with them, Slocum noted. Either that, or he had just developed a humdinger of a tumor in his britches.

He put his hand on the boy's shoulder. "Take Sally, there, first. It's on me."

The kid made a move toward Sally, a cute little redhead who Slocum himself would have picked for himself if Katie hadn't been around. But Slocum tugged him back. "Just the first three times. After that, you pay your own freight, you got me?"

"Gotcha!" Teddy replied, and in an instant, Sally had whisked him up the stairs.

"So that's how it stands," Slocum finished up, and leaned back in his kitchen chair.

"Sounds to me like you're both pretty much stuck," said Katie, sitting opposite him.

Teddy hadn't come up for air yet, but Slocum'd had himself a good feed, courtesy of Katie. *When I should'a been checkin' on my next bounty,* he thought guiltily. The file lay, untouched, inches from his fingers.

Despite what he'd told Teddy—and Katie—he was right annoyed with Pete for saddling him with the kid like this. It wasn't his fault if the man had managed to get himself struck upside the head or something. He had nothing to do with Teddy's fortunate—or unfortunate—memory loss, and now Pete had stuck him with babysitting Teddy for six months?

It not only didn't *seem* fair, it *wasn't.*

No matter, he thought, growling under his breath. *You already gave your word. Sorta. You're stuck.*

But then, he considered that Pete had given him the file, and didn't seem to mind if Teddy went in for a little bounty hunting alongside him. He wasn't so much concerned about Teddy committing another murder, he was just concerned that if he did, it'd be a legal one.

Beside him, Katie said, "Well, you don't need to get so mad about it."

He'd forgotten she was there. He stuttered, "Huh? What?"

"Your body was here, but your mind was somewhere in Upper Egypt," she said, a smile curving her lips.

He realized that there'd been a good reason he'd gifted her with a globe the last time he was through town. He said, "Sorry. I was thinkin'."

She stood up and brushed a kiss over his forehead. "I'll leave you to it, then."

"Thanks, baby," he said, nodding. As she left the room, he picked up his folder and opened it.

Session Bonney, wanted for arson.

Laro Lieberman, wanted for stealing a horse.

Kirk Caruthers, wanted for petty theft.

And on and on. Little stuff with little rewards. He kept turning pages.

At last, he started to get to some high-ticket bad men.

Crane O'Donnell, wanted for robbery and murder. Ticket price, $2500.

Donald Krieger, wanted for rustling and murder at $3000.

Must not've been a very big herd, Slocum thought, smiling a little.

There were rustlers by the dozen, killers by the score. Teddy's paper was in there, too. But one poster stopped Slocum cold.

Washington Trumble, it read. Wanted for murder, train robbery, stagecoach robbery, and kidnapping. $7500, dead or alive.

This looked like something that was more up his alley— and Teddy's, if he started taking to his old ways again.

At least they could shoot this one.

The next morning found them pulling out of Phoenix and heading north, to Ridgeland, where Wash Trumble had been seen last. Four months ago, to be precise. In four months Wash could have gone halfway around the world, but Slocum was hopeful. Most of these boys didn't have that large a frame of reference. In fact, most of 'em didn't even think outside two or three contiguous territories or states.

Additionally, he'd discovered that not only did Teddy know Wash Trumble, but there was bad blood between them. Of course, Teddy wasn't sure why this should be, but just the mention of Wash's name had him good and cranky.

Now, Wash was said to be a big man—over six feet tall, and over two hundred and fifty pounds. He'd had a good education—graduated the eighth grade—and he had a sister up in Flagstaff. These things were both bad and good. The education made him dangerous. The sister made him vulnerable.

He rode alone, to the best of anyone's knowledge. He'd ridden with a gang for the train robbery, but it wasn't his. He'd apparently signed on just long enough for the gang to hold up the Flagstaff Flyer, killing four passengers and three employees in the process of removing over $35,000 from the freight car, along with a number of the passengers' purses, wallets, and jewelry.

Everything Slocum had read about Wash Trumble, in fact, made him seem like a very rough customer. He hoped the stories were more legend than truth, as was so often the case.

In the meantime, Teddy rode quietly along behind him. Almost too quietly, in fact.

Slocum twisted around in his saddle, fully expecting to find Teddy vanished. "You back there, Teddy?"

But the boy was, indeed, right where he was supposed to be, although he didn't look too happy about it.

"Have you ever done this before?" he asked.

"Done what?"

"Kidnappin' an honest citizen and haulin' him—against his will—into an encounter with some dangerous outlaw?"

"Wash Trumble."

"All right, Wash Trumble. What in the hell gives you the right—"

"Plenty," Slocum said. "And I already told you, you'll find out when Pete Stanford decides to tell you."

"But—"

"Now, shut up," Slocum said with finality, and there was no more noise from the peanut gallery.

For a while anyway.

6

That night, they camped in the midlands, where clumps of cholla and prickly pear cactus popped up here in the rolling hills, as might little groves of trees in a milder climate. The next night, they camped higher up. The land that night wasn't craggy yet, but was looking like it was thinking about it. The third night found them sleeping in the mountains, in the early and lowest peaks of the San Francisco range of the Rockies. They'd ride into Ridgeland in the morning.

It had been decades since the last time Slocum was in Ridgeland, and it hadn't been much back then. Just a few houses—more like shacks and lean-tos, really—a mercantile, a sorry excuse for a livery, and a bar. He wondered what it had grown up into. Or grown down into, more like. It looked like most of the silver and gold and copper in the Territory had been mined out. Hell, if Tombstone could die, anything was possible.

Teddy had been quiet—well, quiet for Teddy—over the last few days. Slocum didn't question it. He was just grate-

41

ful. But on this evening, while they were polishing off the last of the coffee, Teddy asked to see the poster of the man they were after.

Slocum nodded, and without a word reached into his pocket and pulled out the paper on Wash Trumble.

Teddy studied it for some time, his face developing from a placid expression into a sneering growl as he read it, then reread it.

He handed it back, and said one word. "Trash."

"And we're here to clean it up."

Teddy stared into his coffee cup. "Said on there that he's killed women and kids."

Slocum nodded. "That's true. In the train robbery."

Again, there was a long silence. Then, again, "Trash."

"Yup," said Slocum, refolding the paper. He was pleased. Pleased that Teddy hadn't jumped to Wash Trumble's defense, pleased that he hadn't come up with something lame, like, *He's my uncle!* Or, *But he saved my dog from drowning when I was a kid!* Nothing showed on his face but hatred.

Slocum said, "I take it that you're up for it."

Teddy set his cup down. "Trash like that doesn't deserve to live. Bad enough, the other stuff he's done, but killin' women and kids?" He shook his head. "That's off the damn scale. Why hasn't somebody brought him in before this?"

Slocum shrugged. He'd asked himself that question time and time again over the years about most every man he'd trailed and apprehended. "What goes around comes 'round. And I guess I'm what you see when it comes back 'round at you."

Teddy managed a brief smile. "Like you're the what-yacall, the harbinger of doom?"

Slocum finished his coffee. "Somethin' like that, I reckon. At least so far. Been lucky."

"So far."

Slocum nodded. "You'd best be lucky, too."

They rode into Ridgeland the next morning at about nine o'clock. Teddy was swiveling his head like a barn owl, watching for Wash. Slocum was more intent on studying the town itself. It had done some growing since he was through. The shacks and lean-tos were gone, having been replaced by honest-to-God houses, made of adobe or wood, sometimes both. The bar had expanded into a full-grown saloon, and the shabby little mercantile had expanded into a street full of shops.

The town wasn't exactly hopping with people, but there were a few folks on the street, going about their business. A wagon was pulled up in front of the new mercantile, and a miner (or so he looked) was loading the wagon's bed with supplies he'd just bought. A few horses, here and there, were tied along the rail. Mostly in front of the saloon, Slocum noted.

When they had ridden down the length of the street, Slocum reined in Ace. Teddy stopped, too.

"What now?"

Slocum reined his horse around. "We go to the sheriff's office." He'd spotted it back up the street. "And then we go to the saloon."

"Why?"

"Why what?"

"Go to the sheriff's office. Or the saloon, for that matter?"

Slocum said as patiently as he could, "We go to the sheriff's office to check in and ask questions. To the saloon to ask questions and get a damn drink. That all right with you?"

Teddy pulled his head back as quick as a water turtle. "Sorry I asked!"

Slocum's expression softened. "My fault. I keep forgettin' this is all new to you."

And I hope the damned sheriff don't up and arrest you, Slocum thought. *That'd be all I need right now, for you to remember who you are and what you done.* But then, he thought, the town may have grown up some, but that didn't necessarily mean it had a lawman worth his salt.

"C'mon," he said, as if he hadn't thought about anything at all.

Everything—at least, everything concerning Teddy— hinged on him not finding out about his own lawless past. For now.

Slocum had been right about the sheriff. He'd been a frail old man who hadn't recognized Teddy, and said he'd never heard of this Wash Trumble character. But he wished them luck and dismissed them.

They rode on up the street and tied their horses outside McBride's Saloon. It was a sight better than the old bar which, as Slocum recalled, didn't even have a bar, just a rough plank set up on a barrel at one end and a sawhorse at the other.

Actually, he sort of missed that old bar. It ran downhill, as he remembered, and if you didn't watch your drink, it was liable to end up dousing the man at the other end.

There were only three other men inside the saloon when Slocum and Teddy walked in. Teddy gave each one a hard look. "He's not in here," he said to Slocum as they sidled up to the bar.

"Couple'a beers," Slocum said to the bartender, and slapped a few coins on the counter. He turned to Teddy. "Did you expect him to be?"

Teddy's brow furrowed. "Well, he could'a been."

"That's right, he could'a. But you walked in here eyein' up these boys like they was all wife scalpers or horse diddlers. That ain't what I call bein' invisible."

The barkeep settled their beers in front of them. Slocum's slid a couple of inches downhill before it came to a rest, and he allowed himself a little smile. No matter how much things changed, some stuff stayed the same.

"Why do I got to be invisible all of a fuckin' sudden?" Teddy demanded, a little too loudly for Slocum's taste.

The barkeep's, too. From the other end of the bar, he hollered, "A little less racket up there, gents."

Slocum tipped his head, indicating that he'd heard. And then he put his face close to Teddy's and whispered, "I dunno how in the hell you managed to live twenty-four whole years without gettin' your fool mouth shot off, but unless you don't wanna live to see twenty-five, you'll keep it shut now. Jesus!" Shaking his head, he took a long pull on his beer, then signaled the bartender for another one.

While he waited, Teddy replied in a whisper, "Stop takin' the Lord's name in vain!"

In surprise, Slocum's brows arched. "What?" he hissed.

"Don't take the Lord's name in vain!" Teddy insisted. He looked like a preacher's kid, who'd just heard it for the first time.

Come to think of if, Teddy *was* a preacher's kid, if he remembered his papers right. *Baptist*, he thought. He wasn't sure how this amnesia thing worked, but he hoped to hell that the kid wasn't going to regress to the diaper stage!

Slocum shook his head. "You are somethin' else, Teddy Cutler," he muttered. He meant it, too.

Just then, he sensed someone coming up behind him, and he wheeled around—to come nose to nose with Wash Trumble.

"Heard somebody was lookin' for me," he growled. "Heard that somebody was you."

He didn't have his gun drawn. His hands were empty. And he was staring Slocum right in the eye.

"Guess you heard right," Slocum said softly, his hand moving, millimeter by millimeter, toward his own holster.

But suddenly, Wash's attention strayed to the kid standing behind Slocum. "Teddy!" Wash roared, and quickly skirted Slocum to grab Teddy by the shoulders. "I wondered what become of you, you li'l ol' scamp!"

"Get your hands off'a me," said a scowling Teddy. "Now!"

Surprised, Wash backed off a foot or two, by which time Slocum had his pistol ready. He buffaloed Wash—banged him over the head with the butt of his gun—and Wash dropped to the floor in a heap.

When Slocum looked up, Teddy was beaming at him. "That sure worked slick!" the kid exclaimed. "I heard the Earps used to use that head bangin' thing all'a the time!"

"You heard right," Slocum said, and holstered his Colt. "You got a rope?"

"For tyin' his hands and such?"

Slocum nodded.

"In a second." Teddy ran outside, to his horse and saddlebags, leaving Slocum—and the saloon's patrons—alone with the slumbering body.

One fellow, sitting alone at a back table, thumbed back his hat and said, "Well, I'll be skinned and hung in the shed for dinner."

"Got that right, Earl," one of the other men said, his head shaking as he spoke. "I never thunk, in a million years, that we'd get shed of Wash Trumble."

"Me neither," echoed his companion.

Those two looked alike, sort of, and Slocum figured them for brothers skipping out on a morning's work.

Teddy showed up with three short lengths of rope, and Slocum set to work hog-tying the unconscious Wash. Once he had the hands bound, he paused and looked over at the brothers. "You boys knew Wash, here, did you?"

Both suddenly struck silent, they bobbed their heads in unison. Slocum turned his attention to the man at the back table. "You, Earl? You know him?"

"I certainly did. And I congratulate you on a fine catch. You know my name, sir. May I have yours?"

Slocum started to tie Wash's ankles, but changed his mind. "Slocum's the name."

"Takin' outlaws's the game!" Teddy piped up, obviously very full of himself, and proud for rhyming.

"Oh, shut the hell up," growled Slocum.

Teddy clamped his jaws for a half second, then took a long swallow of beer before he said, "What do you fellas do up here anyhow? I mean, what keeps the town runnin'?"

"The economy in these parts, young man," said Earl when the brothers froze again, "is based on the mines. Silver and copper, primarily copper, is what's taken from the earth. And I believe there are two cattle ranches as well. Am I right, Clayton?"

One of the two at the other table sat up straight at the mention of his name, and said, "Yessir, Mr. Scrivener, sir."

"Thank you," Earl replied. "However, there won't be two for much longer if the ranch's owner and ramrod continue to spend all their time in town, guzzling beer."

Earl tipped his mug toward Teddy, while, embarrassed, the other two slid money onto the tabletop and quietly departed. Slocum heard their horses gallop away.

"Want some help haulin' him up?" asked Teddy.

"Not yet," replied Slocum, then motioned to the barkeep. "Whiskey this time. A double."

7

Wash woke up two whiskeys and three more beers later, or around noon, depending on how you were counting. Slocum had mellowed out enough that he was counting drinks. It seemed more . . . civilized.

And Earl Scrivener agreed with him. It turned out that Earl was actually an earl. Sort of northern Arizona's answer to Lord Darrell Duppa down Phoenix way, Slocum supposed. Well, the two sure had the booze in common. Earl soaked it up like a sponge, and so did Duppa. Slocum wanted to ask him just how much his family paid him to stay away—Duppa's did, he knew for a fact—but he couldn't quite crank up the nerve, on such short acquaintanceship, to bring up the subject with Earl.

He never found out just what Scrivener was the earl of either, because just as he opened his mouth to ask, Teddy cried, "He's awake!"

Slocum turned toward the voice. Now Teddy'd been watching Wash for signs of life. In fact, he'd dragged a chair across the room and was sitting right over Wash's face. And there was a great big smile on his face, like he'd just won the turkey shoot. Wash twitched and softly groaned at Teddy's feet, not yet fully conscious.

"Give him a few minutes, Teddy," said Slocum.

The brothers had long since vacated the saloon—probably to go tell the know-nothing sheriff all about the goings-on down at the saloon. But the sheriff hadn't surfaced yet.

It was just as well, Slocum thought. He had no intention of parking Wash Trumble in the local jail—where he was likely to get busted out by morning. No sir. He and Teddy were going to pack up Wash and head south, to the marshal's office in Phoenix. If you were going to drop off a killer into custody, that was the best way to do it, Slocum figured.

Course, he hadn't discussed this with Teddy, but he couldn't see the boy giving him any trouble on the matter. Teddy was turning into quite the bounty hunter.

The sound of sloshing water got Slocum's attention again—Teddy had just doused Wash with a glassful. Sputtering, Wash twisted on the floor, trying to get his hands up to wipe off his face. He didn't have any luck, and so rolled onto his back and sat up. "What's goin' on?" he slurred. "What happened?"

"You been caught," Slocum said before the grinning Teddy could get a word out.

But Teddy did manage a soft, "Nyeh, nyeh, nyeh!" which, thankfully, Wash didn't hear. Man! Slocum thought Wash looked like he'd shoot his own ma for a nickel and toss away the change!

Teddy apparently shared his thoughts, because he gave Wash a kick in the ribs with his boot.

Earl slid his beer onto the table. "That should do it," he said softly. He stood up and stepped back from the table.

Slocum should have been more attentive to Earl's motions, but hc wasn't. Wash was tied up, and Teddy had a gun on him. What could Wash do?

Quite a bit, as it turned out. Suddenly, Wash threw himself onto his back and lifted his legs, kicking Teddy in the head. Teddy's gun went sailing to land on the floor on Wash's far side, and Wash immediately started rolling over and over, fast as lightning, to get to it.

But Slocum already had his Colt drawn. He fired it into the floor, just above Wash's rolling head. But Wash's full attention was on his own gun. He'd get to it on the next roll, and Slocum did the only thing he could think to do: He shot Wash, aiming for his shoulder.

Wash was moving too fast, though. The slug caught him high on his back, dead center.

He immediately stopped rolling and landed on his back.

"Aw, shit," said Slocum, and made a face. He'd seen this before, but he hadn't been the cause of it. He hoped he was wrong.

He holstered his gun and went over to Wash, then bent to roll him over on his stomach again. "Aw, crap," he muttered. "Move your legs, Wash."

Nothing.

"Move your arms."

Again, nothing.

Slocum rolled him again, this time onto his back. "Talk to me, Wash."

There was a pause before Wash snarled, "Screw you. Why can't I move nothin'? Whad'ya do to me?"

Slocum backed up to a chair and yanked it out, then sat down on it, backward. "I'm awful sorry, Wash. It was an accident."

"What was an accident, you shithead?"

Earl spoke up. "I believe what Mr. Slocum is trying to

say, Wash, is that he shot you, intending to wound you only. Correct, Slocum?"

Slocum nodded.

"But that unfortunately, you were rolling so fast for the gun that he missed. I believe your spine is severed." Earl gave that a second to settle in, and when it didn't seem to take, he added, "You are paralyzed."

Teddy was still passed out on the saloon floor, Wash's boot having left a red welt on his temple, when the doctor arrived.

Dr. Rush knelt at Wash's side at the same time he said to Slocum, "Throw some water on that man, please. Earl! You didn't tell me it was Wash Trumble!"

"Only because we needed your presence, Doctor," Earl replied. He slid a smile toward Slocum, who was about to douse Teddy with a pitcher of water.

"Wash," Earl went on, "I'm sure you know Zeke Rush, our town doctor. Or at least you've seen him on the street," he added a bit snidely.

Teddy woke up, twisting his head, and gasped, "What's goin' on?"

"You all right?" Slocum asked him.

Teddy's eye landed on the downed Wash, the kneeling doctor, and Earl, standing by. "Fine. What're they doin'?"

"Hush up." Slocum helped him to his feet.

They went over to where the doctor was working on Wash, and pulled out chairs at a nearby table. Teddy asked, "What happened?"

"He was rollin' for your gun, faster than a sidewinder. Thought I was shootin' him in the shoulder, but he was spinnin' too fast. Caught him in the back instead." Slocum shook his head. He had wanted to take Wash in alive and breathing, not strapped to a travois and paralyzed.

"Can he move anything?" Teddy asked, leaning forward.

The doctor turned his head toward Teddy. "Not yet." He turned back to Wash, shaking his head.

Minutes passed, the doctor feeling here and there around the bullet hole, then probing slightly with a medical instrument, periodically asking Wash if he could feel this or that. Wash's answer was always, "No." Then the doctor sat back on his heels with a sigh.

He looked up at Slocum and shook his head. "He won't walk again. Be a miracle if he lasts out the night."

"There someplace we can make him comfortable?" asked Slocum.

Later that afternoon, after they'd hauled Wash to the jail, filled out paperwork for the sheriff, and Slocum had managed to talk to Marshal Pete over the sheriff's office's excuse for a telephone, he and Teddy took themselves, first, to the stable, where they settled in the horses, and second, to the hotel, where they took rooms.

"Don't know if I wanna go over to that saloon again," Teddy declared as he lingered in Slocum's doorway.

"Know whatcha mean," Slocum replied, "but I'm goin' anyways. Only place in town where a man can get a drink, and I need one bad."

Teddy sighed. "All right. I'll go with you."

"We'd best eat, too. Okay?"

"Yeah."

It turned out that the town's only eating establishment was the saloon anyhow, so they each had a fair-to-middlin' roast beef sandwich. Teddy had beans on the side, Slocum had ranch fries. And they both washed it down with a couple of beers. Slocum switched to whiskey the second the plates were taken away.

Now, Slocum had asked Pete to put the full amount of

the reward into his account. He fully intended to give Teddy his fair share, but if the kid all of a sudden got his memory back, Slocum, by God, wasn't going to help him pay for his getaway!

In the meantime, he felt he ought to pay for Teddy's meals and lodging. Seemed fair somehow. So he paid the tab for dinner and signaled the barkeep that he was paying for drinks, too. The barkeep, who had spent most of the afternoon passed out behind the bar in mortal fear of Wash Trumble, nodded skittishly, as if all the meanness that had filled Wash had somehow trickled out and he just hadn't figured who it had gone into yet.

Slocum was in a stoic frame of mind. He didn't feel so bad now about having paralyzed Wash. If Wash died tonight, it'd at least save him having to go to trial, then hang. That was a blessing for both Wash and the taxpayers, he supposed. And if the crowd that filled the saloon tonight was any indication, it was a blessing for the town, too.

The sheriff had suddenly remembered Wash, after they told him Wash would likely die tonight. And Slocum thought he saw a smile hiding behind the man's eyes while he filled out the papers on Wash. The town, it seemed, had been cleansed of a dirty little secret, and it was Slocum who had done the cleansing.

Miner after cowboy after miner after shopkeeper after miner came up to Slocum's table, expressing their thanks and offering their goods or services. Teddy opened his mouth several times at the offers of free merchandise or free services, but Slocum always managed to cut him off with, "Glad to be of service, but no thanks."

Finally, during a break in the proceedings, Slocum said to him, "You can't go acceptin' anythin' from these folks. That'd make you just like Wash. See?"

Teddy sighed and dropped his head to one side. "I

s'pose," he said begrudgingly. "But I bet Wash didn't wait for people to offer him stuff."

Later that night, when the doctor came by to let Slocum know that Wash had passed on, a cheer rose up in the saloon that nearly took the roof off.

Slocum did not participate.

Not much of anyone turned out for Wash Trumble's funeral. They buried him in the town cemetery with little fanfare, although the saloon did a record business once he was put underground for good and all.

And Earl had a marker made of Vermont granite, a tombstone that said:

WASH TRUMBLE
1837–1893
ROBBER, RUSTLER & MURDERER
OF
MEN, WOMEN & CHILDREN.
KILLED BY JOHN SLOCUM,
TO WHOM WE ARE FOREVER INDEBTED.
WITH GRATITUDE,
THE CITIZENS OF RIDGELAND, ARIZONA

Slocum and Teddy were long gone by the time the hurrah built to a roar, however.

Slocum had picked his next mark from the posters in the folder—this one was Homer Crabbe, worth six grand, and last seen up in Flagstaff—and he and the kid had set off after him, to the north.

"Y'know, this is pretty easy, what you do for a livin'," Teddy had remarked when they were halfway to Flagstaff.

Slocum's brow furrowed, but all he said was, "Just you wait, kid. Just you wait."

8

It took them a couple of days to reach Flagstaff, and Teddy, for one, was quite taken with the railhead. Slocum turned him loose for the while it took him to check in with the sheriff, and Teddy had himself a time, crawling around under the cars and looking inside them, and imagining where they'd been and who they'd taken there.

He was a lot more taken with the railway yard than the town, which was sleepy and dusty, despite all the new buildings they seemed to be putting up. But at least they'd have a choice of where to eat and where to drink. He'd seen three cafés and a couple of hotels just coming from the sheriff's office down here.

Speaking of which, he supposed he'd best get up to the depot platform. Slocum was to meet him there. He started hiking back up between the cars.

He still didn't understand what the marshal in Phoenix had against him, to stick him in Slocum's company for six whole months. He was still a little mad, but he had thought

57

and thought, and couldn't remember anything else he was supposed to be doing. And he liked Slocum, so he guessed it wasn't that bad, after all. He liked what they were doing, too! He recalled big ol' Slocum buffaloing Wash upside the head, and grinned. Now, that had been something to see!

A job where all you did was hunt down bad boys and haul them to jail—or kill them and avoid the process entirely? Now, that was a trade he could take to!

He was in a good mood when he gained the platform. There was nobody else there, so he sat down on the bench and rolled himself a smoke. When he lit it and the tobacco filled his lungs, he decided, just like that. He would be a bounty hunter! None'a that "get your kipsack and set out after the strays, Teddy," or "That sidewalk ain't swept half good enough, Teddy," or "Teddy, bring up a jar of pickled eggs." No sir, not for him.

And if he could hang out with Slocum for as long as he'd allow, he could pick up all kinds of tricks of the trade from him. He figured there wasn't anybody better to learn from. And besides, hadn't Slocum seen this deal from both sides? He remembered, when he was a kid, seeing a poster with Slocum's face and a bounty on it, for stealing. He couldn't remember what it was that Slocum had thieved, but it was something big enough to get paper made out on him anyways.

"Teddy?" A strange voice.

But Teddy answered, "Yeah?" anyway. And he looked up to stare directly into the barrel of a long-nosed Smith & Wesson. He gulped, then slowly raised his eyes to peer over the gun's muzzle and into the face of its wielder.

He was shocked.

The voice belonged to a kid, a kid who was sixteen years old if he was a day! He looked mean and ornery, and he was scowling out of a face too big for his bone-thin body. He spoke again. "Get up. No funny stuff."

Slowly, Teddy complied.

"Hands on top'a your head."

Teddy raised his arms, and the boy swiftly relieved him of his Colt. "Look, kid, I dunno what you're thinkin', but I'm here for the U.S. marshal's office, and . . ."

"Shut yer pie hole!" the boy spat. He motioned with Teddy's gun, which he was pointing at Teddy with his left hand. "Now, walk on up the street to the sheriff's office."

Teddy shrugged. "All right, but you're gonna—"

The barrel of one of the guns—the Smith & Wesson, Teddy thought—poked him sharply in the back, and Teddy said, "All right, all right!"

Disgusted, he walked on up to the jail. Boy, was this kid gonna get an earful when they got to Slocum!

"And that's the story, Jethro," Slocum said, rising.

Across the desk, Sheriff Jethro Tanner stood up, too. "Glad you seen fit to check in, Slocum. Save us both some time. You gonna be in town long?"

"Probably just overnight. Gonna check out the ladies," Slocum said with a smile.

Jethro laughed. "If I know you, you're gonna do a lot more than check 'em out."

"Mayhap, may—"

The door burst open, and in walked Teddy, followed by a half-grown kid Slocum didn't recognize. He recognized the gun, though.

Both boys started talking at once.

"I was mindin' my own business when—"

"Have at him, Jethro. It's Teddy Cutler. You can pay me any way you—"

"Pay you?" said Teddy. "I want him thrown in jail for kidnappin'!"

Slocum stepped between them. "Quiet, the both of you!" he shouted.

They both shut up.

Jethro spoke next. "I was afraid a'this. Howdy-do, Teddy." He nodded. "And how you doin', Jack?"

The second lad said, "Not too damn well, Jethro! I said, this here's Teddy Cutler! I found him down at the train station, rollin' a cigarette and sittin' on the bench like he owned the whole place!"

Jethro slipped his arm around Jack's shoulders. "I wanna have a little talk with you, Jack. In private. Meantime . . ." He slid Teddy's gun from Jack's hand, and held it out to Teddy.

Jack shouted, "Hey!"

"In private, Jack," Jethro said, and turned Jack back toward his desk and chairs. Over his shoulder, he said, "Thanks again, Slocum. See you, Teddy."

"But, Jethro . . ." the boy began as Slocum, ushering Teddy before him, closed the door and started down the darkening street.

"What the hell was *that* about?" Teddy demanded. He was as hot as a roasted rattler on a plate full of peppers.

"Ain't about you," Slocum lied. "It's about Jack. He's a local—a half-cracked local—who fancies himself a bounty hunter. Imagine that right about now, Jethro's tellin' him to leave us alone."

"But how'd he know my name?"

Slocum shrugged. "Hard tellin'. Who knows? Now, let's go get us some dinner!"

"But—"

"Jethro says they got fresh crabs in on the four-ten from Portland over at the Red Curtain Café," Slocum said. "You got a taste for seafood?"

Teddy kicked at a rock in the road. "Don't know. Never had any'a them sea-bugs."

"Well, what'd you say you try 'em tonight?"

"Fine."

"Good!"

After checking in at the hotel and bedding down the horses, the two took themselves up to the Red Curtain Café. The place wasn't packed, but they were doing a pretty fair business. Slocum looked around. Most of the diners were chowing down on platters of crab, so they were in the right place. He said, "Hope they ain't sold outta the stuff," as he and Teddy took a table.

Teddy had started in again—about how in the hell Jack had known his name—down at the stable, but Slocum had just shrugged his shoulders and told Teddy that he didn't know, and to shut up about it already.

Teddy had taken him at his word, although grudgingly, and hadn't uttered another word about it. Thank God.

They sat at a table toward the back of the restaurant, and it wasn't but a few minutes before a waiter brought them menus. Slocum, however, waved his away.

"Beer to drink, and crab," he said. "Lots of it."

The waiter scribbled on a notepad, then said, "Potatoes or rice?"

"What kinda potatoes you got?"

"Fritters, hash browns, mashed, baked, and cottage fried."

Slocum nodded. "Baked. With sour cream, if you got any."

The waiter allowed that they did. "Vegetable? We have carrot casserole, three-bean salad, fresh garden peas, white corn on the cob—"

"Corn. And green salad, with vinegar and oil dressing."

The waiter made a final note on his pad, then turned toward Teddy, who had been studying the menu. He handed it over. "I'll take what he's havin'." After the waiter left,

Teddy added, "It's easier than goin' through that whole dang thing again."

Slocum nodded. "You're a wise man, Teddy. Now, just you wait. You're in for a treat!"

Dinner was served, and while Slocum wasted no time digging into his crab, Teddy just sat there, staring at his.

Slocum noted his lack of enthusiasm, and said, "You gotta crack the shell." He held up his crab cracker, and Teddy reluctantly picked up his. Slocum demonstrated how to work it, then showed Teddy how to dip the meat in the clarified butter the waiter had brought.

Once Teddy actually had his first mouthful of crab, his whole face lit up like Christmas. "By Christ!" he said, once he was capable of speech. "This is the best dang stuff I ever ate. And when I say ever, I mean in all my born days!"

He dove in, and didn't speak another word for the rest of the meal. Slocum was glad. Not only for the silence, but for the reprieve—he wasn't in the mood to answer any more uncomfortable questions, or to discuss their next quarry. This one was going to take a lot longer than Wash Trumble— what didn't?—and he was in no mood to explain his reasoning to Teddy.

At least, when they were out on the trail, he wouldn't run into any fool kid bounty hunters. Maybe, with his attention diverted by the struggles of the trail, Teddy would forget about the one he'd met today.

After they'd finished their dinner—and a dessert of chocolate cake—they repaired to the hotel. Teddy stopped at Slocum's door and shifted from foot to foot.

"All right, Teddy," Slocum said. "C'mon in." The kid did, and shut the door behind him. "What's on your mind?"

Teddy sat down in the stuffed chair opposite the bed, then sat forward, elbows on knees. "Been thinkin', Slocum."

"Always a bad sign," Slocum muttered beneath his breath before he looked over at Teddy. "What 'bout?"

"I remembered some stuff."

Slocum tried like hell to keep the frown off his face, but had little luck. "What kind'a stuff?"

Teddy shook his head. "It's all kind'a . . . disjointed, y'know? Little bits an' pieces'a things, things you'd see in some play."

Slocum arched a brow. "You remembered goin' to a play?"

"No, damn it. It's like it's my life, but it isn't. It's . . . Aw, hell. I'm not 'splainin' myself too good." He put his head in his hands and held it, rocking slowly back and forth.

Slocum, against his wiser leanings, took a little pity on the boy. He walked over and put his hand on Teddy's shoulder. "One reason Marshal Pete chained us together like this? It's because you had a little trouble with your memory down to Phoenix. You remember that?"

Muffled, Teddy said, "Yeah."

"Good. You were having trouble rememberin' stuff from some time back, too. It was kinda like somebody took hold'a your brain and wiped it clean."

Teddy looked up. "For how long?"

"We don't know. Seems you got a little of it leakin' through now, though." He patted Teddy's shoulder before he moved away. "You'll be all right, kid."

Quietly, Teddy stood up and opened the door. "Thanks, Slocum," he muttered before he went out into the hall. "See you in the mornin'."

Slocum was alone before he said, "Night, kid," and went back out again, this time on the hunt for some female companionship.

9

The next morning, Slocum shook Teddy out of bed at around eight, and they made off after Homer Crabbe's trail. Or at least, the sheriff's best guess at it, a path that would take them into the mountains to the west.

Slocum didn't know Crabbe, didn't know anything about him, other than what was printed on the poster: He was wanted for horse theft, arson, and two incidental murders, so Slocum made a mental note to watch out for this one. He was purported to carry a Sharps carbine rifle and double rigged Colts—those, Slocum wore himself—and was reported to travel with an Arkansas toothpick in his right boot.

He was obviously a man you didn't want to meddle with unless you had a damn good reason. Slocum figured that the six grand on Homer's head was reason enough. But as he and Teddy rode along through the pine forest, ducking limbs and looking for the trail, he wondered if the boy was ready for it. Teddy was cocky enough, but that was based on their luck with Wash Trumble. They weren't going to be that lucky again.

He was about to open his mouth and start a conversation about it, but Teddy, riding ahead, beat him to the punch. "Slocum?" he called back, reining in his horse, "I just can't figure it out. 'Bout that kid knowin' my name and all. How you 'spose he did that anyways?"

Slocum rode up next to him and stopped, too. He ran a cuff over his brow and said, "Teddy, I don't know. I told you and told you. How many more times I gotta keep tellin' you?"

Teddy colored a little, but managed to say, "Don't you even think it's kind'a funny? I mean, how many times does a feller come up to you and say, 'You're Slocum and I'm takin' you in!'"

This inadvertently caused Slocum to smile a little. "Quite a few, actually."

Teddy pounded his knee with his fist. "Aw, that's a rotten example. I never done anything to make me a wanted man, but I seen paper on you when I was a kid. For thievin' somethin'."

Slocum chuckled. "Remember what it was?"

"No. But I'm makin' the point that I ain't never done nothin' to make me wanted. By anybody!" Teddy was adamant.

"Don't go yellin' at me," Slocum said. "I didn't have nothin' to do with it." He looked past Teddy's left shoulder, then pointed a finger along his line of sight. "There's the trail over there."

Teddy twisted to look, then twisted back. "Well," he said, reining his horse around, "I just don't get it."

"That's life," Slocum said. "Get used to it. And I wanted to talk to you about somethin' else. This man we're goin' after, this Homer Crabbe."

"Six thousand!" Teddy said happily, then made a sound something like a cash register's clang. "We're gonna be so rich, Slocum!"

"You say that like it's a done deal," Slocum replied. They were on the trail now, and it had been beaten down enough that they could ride side by side. "It ain't. The sheriff back in Flag gave me quite a rundown on Homer Crabbe, and he's one dangerous sonofabitch. I think mayhap we should go after one'a the others first, maybe two or three. Y'know, just to kind'a get you broke in. What'd'ya say?"

Teddy looked surprised, and a little angry that Slocum would have to even think such a thing! He said, "We already done that. Broke me in, I mean. On Wash Trumble."

Slocum's head shook. "Not even halfway. Ol' Wash was a sack'a sugar candy, compared to Homer. Hell, compared to your average six-year-old!"

"Nope, no way. Nobody else in that file you got pays as good as Homer. So long as you gotta take me along, I figure I should get a say in who we go after." He stopped talking for a moment to duck beneath an overhanging pine branch. "And you already had your say. You're the one that picked him out in the first place!"

Slocum was silent. The kid did have a point. He was just afraid that if he let Teddy have his way, he was going to wind up dead. Hell, maybe they'd both get killed.

But for now, he held his peace. The kid was stirred up right now. He'd let Teddy simmer in his own juices for a bit.

Come nightfall, they bedded down in a clearing that had once been a beaver pond. Slocum staked the horses out in the center so they could graze to their hearts' content, while he and Teddy bedded down nearer the trees and built a fire.

Slocum brought out some of the grub he'd bought while

they were in Flag, and began to put together a stew for their dinner while Teddy made coffee. Teddy made good coffee. Slocum had left that part to him from the first time he'd made it after they left Phoenix.

He was cutting up an onion for the stew when, out of the blue, Teddy said, "How long you figure? I mean, till we find him."

Slocum gave a shrug. "Could be tomorrow, could be three or four months. He's a cagy one."

"Three or four *months*?" Teddy looked like he'd been struck by lightning. "You joshin' me?"

"Could be longer. Nobody knows where he is." Slocum finished with the onion and tossed it in the pot with the beef he'd bought. He picked up a potato and began slicing.

Teddy muttered, "Three or four months. Months!" and flopped back on his bedroll. Louder, he said, "I wish he'd ride in here tonight, and we could jus' shoot him! I mean, he's wanted dead or alive, ain't he? God damn it anyhow!"

Slocum dumped the spud in the pot, then picked up another to slice. Quietly, he said, "Well, I don't think that's gonna happen. I ain't got that kind'a luck. And apparently neither do you."

Teddy grunted out something that escaped Slocum, but it was obvious that Teddy had been thinking again: usually a bad sign, but in this case, it might actually be to both their benefits.

Slocum kept his mouth shut, and kept on slicing potatoes. Quiet was the best way to deal with Teddy. For now. Later on, if he didn't change his mind about their quarry, he might have to slap the kid around a little.

But after a while, long after Slocum had taken the cooked stew off the fire, after they'd finished the meal in silence and sat, drinking coffee, Teddy finally said, "Aw, I s'pose we could go after one'a them cheaper guys. Maybe two or three of 'em. What'd you think?"

Slocum looked over the rim of his coffee cup at Teddy. The kid seemed sincere enough. The silent treatment had worked, all right. He took a long drink of coffee before he answered, just to keep the amusement out of his voice.

"Think you're makin' a good point, Teddy. Go for the smaller ticket boys. They'd add up to six thousand bucks soon enough. And if we just happen to cross paths with ol' Homer . . ." He stopped to shrug. "Well, we'll just consider it the hand of fate. I'm okay with that if you are."

Teddy nodded, his face brightening somewhat. Actually, he looked relieved. "That's settled, then. Now, who do we go after next?"

This time, Slocum let the chuckle out, and Teddy, although he looked a little puzzled at first, joined in.

The next morning brought them a later start than the last. There were posters to go through and argue over, breakfast to be made and eaten, and Teddy's mare had found the stream's leftover mudhole during the night and rolled in it.

They didn't leave the clearing until their quarry was picked, their bellies were full, and Teddy's mare was groomed into her original condition.

The man they had chosen to look for was one Jorge Ruiz, wanted for murder, assault, and horse theft. The poster said he was worth $1500, alive only. Slocum kept on repeating that last bit to Teddy—all he needed was for Teddy to kill somebody else right now, when he had a path to freedom. Chances like that came along once in a blue moon, and Slocum was going to do his damnedest to make certain Teddy didn't blow it.

Young Jorge had murdered a prostitute (Jorge said she

was, her family said she wasn't) down around Tucson, then beat up the deputy sheriff who'd taken him into custody, and stolen a horse—which just happened to be the mayor's— on the way out of town. The last time anybody had seen him was on the date of the crime, last June fourteenth. Three months ago. Which meant he could be just about anywhere.

But Slocum was happy with the odds. Jorge had headed out of town, going north, in a big hurry. Chances were that he'd turned west to follow the old Mormon Trail. Slocum doubted he'd go up to Phoenix, especially now that things were booming up there.

But he felt that a trip through Phoenix was excusable. The little Mexican whore he'd picked up the other night hadn't been any too talented, and he had a hankering for somebody with more . . . spice to her lovemaking. So in his mind, they were headed for Katie's.

Now, what was on Teddy's mind was anybody's guess. He'd been uncharacteristically quiet all morning—except for the time he discovered his mare had rolled in the mud, of course. When that happened, all manner of cuss words came from him that you wouldn't expect a preacher's kid to know. But after that, not a word.

By afternoon, they were down into the foothills and leaving the tall pines behind. They'd gnawed on jerky and hardtack for lunch, so that they could keep moving south, but by a little before nightfall, Slocum had shot a couple of jackrabbits, planning on rabbit stew for supper.

They stopped and made camp in the open, in a place where the green fields went rolling on forever, frequently punctuated by stands of prickly pear and jumping cholla. It must have rained pretty damn good up here, thought Slocum, and recently, for the grasses to have got so thick and green.

As usual, Teddy made a fire and started making coffee

while Slocum cut up the rabbits and began slicing and dicing the vegetables. They ate their dinner in silence—normal for Slocum, but not for Teddy—and finally, when their plates were empty and they were both sitting, sipping coffee, Slocum paused to take a draw on his cigarette.

The smoke rolled out as fast as it had been taken in, and he asked, "What you plannin' on doin' in Phoenix?"

Teddy looked up. "That where we're headed?"

"I'm thinkin' Monkey Springs to start with, but Phoenix is on the way."

Teddy slowly shook his head. "No it ain't, if we go like the crow flies."

Slocum smiled a little. "Crows don't need to be stoppin' in at no whorehouses, kid."

"Oh," Teddy said, nodding. "Miss Katie?"

"Yeah. And you can have your pick of the others. That be okay with you?"

Teddy wasn't shy with his smiles. "You betcha! But we ain't stoppin' long, right?"

"Right. But why're you in such a hurry?"

"I wanna get Jorge!"

Slocum chuckled. The kid was still bound to him by the promise of bounty money, and wasn't likely to take off in the middle of the night. Or the middle of the day, for that matter.

10

After two more days on the trail, they entered Phoenix again. The place was undergoing a lot of change, and new folks were moving into town all the time.

"We'd best be checkin' in with the marshal, first thing," Slocum said after they'd forded one of the old irrigation canals that ran between them and the capital's downtown.

"How come?" asked Teddy. "And why don't they build themselves some'a those dang bridges?"

"Because I feel like it's what I should do. And they are." Slocum pointed down the long canal a ways, where men were at work spanning the water. "You wanna go see?" Actually, Slocum wouldn't have to be talked into it at all. He liked watching men build things, especially when there was no chance he'd be asked to lend a hand.

Teddy nodded, and they set off down the bank toward the crew.

"You know the story?" Slocum asked. "I mean, you know how the canals got here and everything?"

Teddy shrugged. "Somebody dug 'em, I reckon."

"Yup. A real long time ago, before anybody out here had heard of white people. Before the white people even knew that this continent existed."

"Aw, you're joshin' me!"

Slocum shook his head. "Nope, no josh. There was a tribe of Indians that lived here. Called the Hohokam. Well, I don't know what they was called exactly, 'cause they was named by one of the other tribes. 'Hohokam' means the 'Lost Ones,' or the 'Vanished Ones,' somethin' like that. Anyhow, they dug the valley full'a irrigation canals."

"Wait a second," Teddy interjected. "How come they took off after they done all that work?"

"Nobody knows," Slocum said with a shrug. "And nobody knows where they went either. Let's stop here, and we can watch 'em from the shade." They stopped beneath a huge cottonwood, dismounted, and sat on the ground. Slocum took a swig from his canteen, then began to roll himself a quirlie. That was another reason to be stopping in Phoenix—he had a hankering for a couple packs of ready-mades.

"Well, if no white man seen 'em, maybe they didn't exist in the first place," Teddy said offhand.

"You think white men are the only ones to trust with history? Hell, I knew a colored man who could tell you all the names of his ancestors, back ten generations' worth. Met a few Chinese who could do it, too. Could you do that?"

Teddy stared at his lap. "Well, no. I guess you gotta point."

"Damn right, I do." Slocum finally lit his quirlie. It was good enough for a quirlie, but he wanted ready-mades something crazy! "Anyhow, there's places where men dug up a whole lot of old pottery and stuff. They even found an old ball court somewhere outside'a town."

"A what?"

"You know, where they had organized ball games and such. No," he responded to Teddy's scowl, "not like baseball. Hell, nobody knows for sure. But I heard from a feller that there's old Indian ruins down in southern Mexico where they got the same thing. The old ball courts, I mean."

Teddy looked him square in the eyes. "You're as goonie as a mustang on loco weed!"

Slocum blurted out a laugh. "Believe me or not, it's the truth. Your choice."

Teddy just shook his head, obviously thinking that he'd been riding with a lunatic for the last week and a half.

Slocum rolled himself another quirlie, and they sat in silence, watching the workers build the bridge. They were building one wide enough to support a good-sized buckboard, and they weren't going to finish today, so once he put out his quirlie, he stood up and stretched. "Better get goin', Teddy," he said. "Gonna be dark pretty soon."

Teddy didn't reply, and when Slocum bent down to him, he was sound asleep.

Guess I ain't the most thrillin' company, Slocum thought, and gave Teddy a shake.

The boy came to almost instantly, grumbling, "What? Who's it?" Then he recognized his surroundings and apologized. "Sorry, Slocum. Guess I kinda nodded off."

"Kinda?" Slocum said, grinning a little.

Teddy hauled himself up off the ground. "All right! I went t'sleep. You wanna whip me through the streets? Toss me in jail? Beat me silly?"

"No. Just want you to get on your mare."

"Fine!" Teddy snarled, embarrassed and trying to cover it with anger. He swung himself up into the saddle with one hand and sat there, pouting.

Slocum remembered when he could do that. Swing up

into the saddle, he meant. These days, his legs weren't up to it. He mounted Ace with surety, though, and said, "First the marshal's office. Then we gotta stop at the tobacconist's."

"The what?"

"The store with the wooden Indian out front."

"Oh," Teddy replied, somewhat chagrined. "You gonna buy yourself one'a them big expensive Cuban cigars? To celebrate?"

They began riding toward town. "No, just some ready-mades. But that cigar thing, that's a good idea. Think you deserve one, too!"

Teddy's face lit up. "Sounds great!"

Later, that evening, they were both settled in at Katie's place, the horses were safely tucked in at the livery stable, and Slocum was downstairs, listening to the piano player beat out the old songs and to the seductive chatter of a couple of the girls and their clients-to-be, and smoking a fine Havana.

Leaning back in his comfortable chair—and knowing Teddy was safely ensconced upstairs with one of the girls—he thought back on the day. It had been an easy ride, he'd got to stop and watch men build a bridge, and the marshal had been real easy to get along with. He'd reported in on Teddy—saying as how he'd remembered some stuff, but nothing incriminating, and that so far, he'd showed no signs of wanting to take off. In fact, he was excited and eager to be off after the next fugitive.

"I'm teachin' him a trade, I reckon," Slocum had said with a grin.

"Yup, I believe you are." Marshal Pete had grinned back at him. "Good work, Slocum. And your money's in the bank."

Slocum stood up. "Never doubted you, Pete." He shook

hands with Pete, and then left to pick up Teddy, who he knew was impatiently awaiting him in the outer office.

He did, and the two of them had set off for the tobacconist's. Slocum bought two of the best Havanas they had in stock—rolled on the tender, sweaty thighs of Cuban girls, then soaked in the best rum, and left to dry before being packaged and shipped to the United States.

God bless free trade, he thought, then took another puff. The smoke was almost better than sex. Not quite, but almost. He chuckled under his breath.

Then he reached to the side table and picked up his glass. Champagne. He hadn't forgotten anything. They'd been real obliging to him at the saloon, too. They likely didn't have too many customers for this fancy French stuff— not at a hundred dollars a bottle anyway—but he was enjoying every single sip.

"Slocum! When'd you get back?" One of the girls—Iris, he thought—had just bade her customer good-bye at the front door. She brushed long, dark hair away from her fair-skinned face and sleepy, deep brown, bedroom eyes.

"'Bout an hour ago," he said, smiling. If it weren't for Katie, he'd take Iris in a slap second!

"Seen Katie?" she asked.

"Nope. Mandy, there," he said, pointing at the little red-head sweet-talking a banker-type across the room, "said she was out runnin' a couple of errands. Oughta be back anytime now."

"Well, it don't look like much is goin' on out here," Iris said. "Think I'll get myself a cup of coffee." And with that, she disappeared down the back hall.

Mighty fine, Slocum thought. *Mighty fine.*

And then he heard conversation coming from the kitchen. Iris's voice, and Katie's. He started to stiffen at just the sound of her voice, and took another drink of his champagne, reminding himself to save some for Katie. She appreciated a good glass of the bubbly, too.

In no time, he heard footsteps coming up the hall and turned his head just in time to see Katie emerge into the front room. She cried, "Slocum!" and bent to kiss him before she perched on the ottoman in front of his chair. "I'm surprised to see you so soon! Are your visits gonna get more frequent?" There was a distinctly hopeful tone to her voice.

So he said, "Maybe so, Katie. Hard to tell, though, what with leadin' Teddy around. You hear? We got Wash Trumble."

Katie laughed. "Did I hear? It's been all over town! You're a hero all over again!"

"Didn't know I was ever one in the first place," Slocum said, self-effacingly, and shrugged. "C'mon, Katie. Get yourself a glass." He pointed to the champagne bottle.

She leaned forward until he was looking deep into her cleavage, and kissed him on the mouth. "I'd be delighted, Mr. Slocum!" Then, giggling, she was up and off to the kitchen.

Down, boy, down, Slocum thought, looking at his lap. If Katie kept this up, they were going to have to make love right here, in front of everybody.

That thought managed to back him down a bit, and he relaxed again and took another puff on his cigar.

Then again, he thought, *maybe we oughta get a head start on it.*

He stood up, bringing both the champagne glass and bottle with him and began to mosey over toward the staircase. Just as he reached the first step, Katie appeared.

"That's what I like about you, Slocum," she said, linking her arm through his. "We think alike."

As they walked upstairs, she said, "Oh, I forgot to tell you somethin'."

"What?"

"You recall that gal that was here before, when you were?"

"Which one?" It'd be kind of hard to remember, in a town with almost a thousand women in it!

"That one you said was a bounty hunter? Pretty little blond thing? Miss . . . Miss . . . Miss . . . Alice Swan! I knew it was in my brain. Just a matter'a knockin' it out."

"What about her?" They had reached her room, and Slocum, ever the gentleman, opened the door for Katie. He didn't want to think about Alice Swan right now. He just wanted to get inside and get Katie free of that corset.

"I saw her yesterday. Today, too. I thought it was funny that she'd be back in town so quick."

That got Slocum's attention. "She's back? What the hell for?"

Katie shrugged and held forth her empty glass. While Slocum filled it, she replied, "Damned if I know. I even asked her. But I guess she's one'a those highfalutin gals that don't have any truck with my sort. I didn't get nothin' more from her than a 'thank you, and good day,' and by the time I thought of somethin' good an' cuttin' to answer back, she was across the street and goin' in the hotel." She chugged back her champagne. "Hey, this is the good stuff!"

11

By the next morning, Slocum was a new man. Not only had Katie liked the champagne, but she'd gone loopy on it and bucked beneath him like a wild bronco all night long. He stopped counting when she came for the fifth time, but he knew that he came four times.

He was a very happy man, and so this morning, it was time that he went to see Miss Alice Swan. At least he figured he'd best already be in a good mood to see her. If he hadn't had such a spirit-lifting encounter with Katie last night, he'd have likely killed Miss Alice Swan right off the bat, by way of saying good morning.

He arrived at the hotel at about nine-thirty, and asked for her at the desk, where the clerk told him she'd stepped out.

Bloody hell. Was he gonna have to trail her all over town?

But when he stepped out over the hotel's threshold, he looked across the street and saw her coming out of the mar-shal's office. She was headed for the hotel, so he simply moved over a couple of feet on the boardwalk and sank down on one of the hotel's benches. He stayed there, looking down, until she had come up the street, crossed over, and was practically on top of him.

Suddenly, he stood up, causing her to gasp and step back. He touched the brim of his hat. "Miss Swan," he said. "Bring in a bounty, did you?"

"I'm sure I don't have the slightest idea what you're talking about, Mr. Slocum," she sniffed.

Why didn't she want him to know that she'd been at Pete's office? Odd. He tried again. "Now, Miss Swan, we both know I seen you come outta the marshal's office. What were you doin' in there?"

She stuck her nose up into the air. "I can't see as how that's any of your business."

Slocum huffed out a little sigh, and pulled himself up to his full height. Staring down at her, he growled, "We both know it *is* my business, Alice. In fact, it's *mostly* my business, and you're the dog caught with his nose up the wrong bitch. I trust you'll pardon my language," he added snidely.

She glared at him for a long minute, then finally she said, "I was simply checking on the status of young Mr. Cutler," she said between clenched teeth. "I was informed that he is under control. For the time being." She tipped her head. "And I suppose I should tell you congratulations for bringing down Washington Trumble. Word has it that it only took one shot."

All the stone and starch went out of him. He wasn't proud of the way Wash had died. He doubted Wash was either.

"That's done with," he said curtly. "And Teddy's gonna keep on doin' just fine. He'd a good kid, just got off-track somewhere along the line, that's all. Leave him be, Alice."

That last sentence had almost been a plea. He knew—or

at least, he was pretty sure—that if Alice Swan got hold of Teddy and started tellin' him all the stuff he'd done, and about the folks he'd killed, Teddy'd start to remember for sure and certain. And he'd be off to a life of crime all over again. Except that this time, she'd be there to catch him. If he didn't kill her first.

She clasped her hands behind her back. "I will consider it, Mr. Slocum." Complete ambivalence. Neither her face nor her posture gave any evidence which way she was leaning.

Although he figured that it wasn't the way he wanted, if her past performance counted for anything.

"Good day, then, Miss Swan," he said, touching the brim of his hat again. Then he stalked off, down the street, to where women knew their place.

Katie's.

But first, the tobacconist's. He needed another cigar.

"Well, if we ain't leavin' today, when *are* we goin'?" Teddy demanded over a cold lunch of meats, cheeses, sliced tomatoes, and warm, oven-fresh bread.

"How come you're all of a sudden in such a big toot, Teddy?" Slocum asked. "What happened? Did that little gal'a yours kick you out?"

Teddy's head pulled back like an insulted turtle's. "She wouldn't do no such thing! It's just . . . just that I got this feeling, this feeling that Jorge's close, real close. We don't move now, we might never catch him!"

Slocum nodded. The famous feeling. He'd had it himself a few times. Well, it was a chance to try the kid's instincts out.

Slocum finished chewing his last bite of sandwich, and swallowed before he said, "Tomorrow mornin' soon enough for you?"

Teddy's face lit up. "Perfect!"

"All right. That's it, then."

Teddy had finished his lunch already, and whooping, hauled his little gal to her feet and ran her up the stairs.

From beside Slocum came Katie's voice. "Tomorrow? Really?" When he turned toward her, she looked ready to burst into tears.

"Now, Katie, I about got to," he said, putting a hand on her leg. "We'll be back through town, I promise."

"You really mean it?"

He held up two fingers. "Step on a crack, break my mama's back."

Katie smiled. "All right, you big ol' scamp."

"You're awful pretty when you do that."

"Do what?"

"Smile," he said, and pulled her face closer so that he could kiss it.

She was really one hell of a beautiful woman. All rosy and fair at the same time with that little spatter of freckles over her delicate nose, that beautiful silky red, Titian hair, and that knockout body . . . he found himself wanting to stay over another week. Or longer.

But now he'd given his word to Teddy, and he was honor-bound to keep it. Besides, the kid might really have a good sense for this sort of thing. And there was no way to test it, except to go.

He broke off the kiss, punctuating it with a little peck to the tip of her nose, and turned his attention to his lunch again. "You know, don't you," he said, picking up his sandwich again, "that you make it pretty damned hard on a feller."

She giggled, and he quickly said, "Aw, you know what I mean. You make it hard for me to leave, just bein' your-self."

"And you're a sweet-talker, darlin'," she said softly as she rose. "I gotta run upstairs for a second." She looked across the table toward Iris and Belle. "You girls take care'a him till I get back."

Iris's brows shot up. It seemed like everybody was taking everything wrong today. Smiling, she asked, "Do you mean . . . ?"

But her face fell again when Katie scowled at her and said, "No. I certainly do not!"

Slocum hid a grin and chuckled beneath his breath as he took another bite of his sandwich. He guessed he'd never get a chance to get in Iris's pants as long as Katie was around. But surprisingly, it didn't bother him. Katie was all the woman a man could ask for.

The next morning, he and Teddy saddled up and headed off toward Monkey Springs. It was a tiny town—not much more than a wide spot on the road, really—west of Tucson, but still about three days' ride to the California border.

Slocum hoped that Teddy's sixth sense wasn't letting him down. He wanted to get this over with as soon as humanly possible and get back to Phoenix. Which was odd. He wasn't much one for towns or people, generally speaking. But that Katie, she sure had him on a short leash, metaphorically speaking. And he'd be damned if he knew how it got there.

"How far are we now?" came a voice from behind him. Christ, he'd almost forgotten about Teddy!

He said, "A little less far than the last time you asked. Like I already told you—what, three times?—we'll get there around nightfall. And it's only . . ." He dipped fingers into his pocket to dig out and peer at his watch. "It's only ten-thirty. Okay?"

A surly Teddy replied, "Yeah," and said no more. Slocum could still hear his horse's hoofbeats following along behind, so the possibility that he'd take flight was pretty slim. It wasn't out of the question, though. It was a possibility of which Slocum was extremely aware. So he reminded himself to pay attention to the hoofbeats, and stay on his toes.

At noon, they stopped to rest the horses and take some lunch. Katie had taken care of them, all right. She'd sent them off with a whole roasted chicken, a hunk of the cheddar that Slocum liked so much, a loaf of bread—baked fresh that morning, and sliced and buttered—half a dozen boiled eggs, half an apple pie, and a bowl of potato salad. She'd said they ought to eat the potato salad first thing so it wouldn't have a chance to go bad, so Slocum fixed himself and the boy each a tin plate with potato salad and chicken sandwiches.

Teddy brewed the coffee, as usual.

For God-only-knew-what reason, Ace had been whickering and begging for some of that potato salad, so when they were finished eating, Slocum gave him the last of it. Slocum imagined that they made quite a sight standing out there in the middle of the backside of creation—a beat-up ol' cowboy holding a blue and white porcelain bowl while a wild-colored Appy licked it clean of potato salad.

Teddy echoed his thoughts. "Wish I had one'a those camera rigs with me. You'd make quite a picture right 'bout now."

Slocum laughed. "Reckon I would, Teddy," he said while he let Ace take the last few licks. About all he was getting now was blue paint off the porcelain.

Teddy was cleaning up the camp so they could move out again. That was one good thing about him—he sure wasn't a shirker. He was always up, always awake, always ready for anything. Well, maybe anything except a potato salad–eating horse.

Slocum took the bowl away while it still had some color left, and packed it up with the rest of their gear. Then it was off into the scrub, where he took a long piss before, buttoning up his pants, he walked back into camp.

Teddy was already mounted. "I already snugged your horse's girth," he said before Slocum had a chance to check.

"You water 'em?" Slocum asked, one hand on the canvas water bag.

"When we first stopped," Teddy said. "Don'cha recall?"

"Oh, yeah," Slocum said before he mounted Ace and started off, south. "Sorry. Slipped my mind."

"You ain't gonna go all senile on me, are you?"

"Jesus! I ain't that old, boy!" But he was thinking, *Lord, maybe I am!*

"Don't get snappish with me," Teddy said. "I never could tell how old anybody was." He looked over. "How old are you anyway?"

It was all Slocum could do not to leap off Ace and onto Teddy's mare and smack him alongside the head. Maybe knock him to the ground. But he didn't. He just growled, "None'a your goddamn business," and Teddy had the sense to let the subject lie.

By the time he could see the northern tip of the Santa Rita range, he and Teddy had ridden at least three more hours, some of that at a slow gallop and all of it in silence. Slocum gave them another couple of hours before they rode on into Monkey Springs.

They'd made good time.

12

When they rode into Monkey Springs that evening, even the dying light couldn't disguise that they'd ridden into practically a ghost town. The general store was still standing as well as what passed for a saloon, but the old livery had collapsed in on itself and nobody had even bothered to clear up the boards.

Teddy's head twisted all around, like a barn owl's. "You *sure* this's a town?" he asked, breaking the long silence.

"Thought you'd been here before," Slocum said, dismounting.

"No," Teddy corrected him, "I just said I reckoned I knowed where it was. And it's right here, too! Or at least, the leftovers."

"Leftovers is about right." Slocum tied his horse to the rail out front of the saloon. "Get down. We can get a drink anyway."

They had watered the horses about a half hour before they came riding into Monkey Springs, so they were content to be tethered to the rail. Slocum led Teddy into the saloon.

That, at least, hadn't changed. It was still narrow, with stools at the bar and no tables to den up around. And it was empty, except for one lonely bartender, who said, "Welcome, fellers! Come on in!" when they first parted the batwing doors.

"Can I getcha some wet for your whistles?" he asked, not a second later.

When they both said, "Beer," he set off toward the taps.

"Why're we even stoppin' here?" asked Teddy.

Slocum snorted. "Don't go quizzin' me. You're the one what got a wild hare up his butt about the town."

Teddy just made a face, probably out of embarrassment.

The bartender came back and slid two beers in front of them. Slocum reciprocated by pulling a couple of coins from his pockets. "You get much trade around here?" he asked the man.

The barkeep held his hand out level, then moved it from side to side. "Now an' then, now an' then."

"S'pose you'd recall a stranger, then?"

"Don't know." The bartender raised his brows. "Maybe I would."

Slocum sighed. This one was going to take some greasing. He brought out another coin—a double eagle that sparkled in the lamplight—and held it in his palm. The barkeep's eyes instantly locked onto it.

"Did you have a young Mexican feller come through, oh, 'bout three months back?"

"Sure. Lots'a Mexicans come through."

"This one was called Jorge. Jorge . . ."

"Ruiz," Teddy said, his voice overly eager. "Jorge Ruiz."

"Yeah, that's it." Slocum nodded, but slid his leg over to

knee Teddy in the thigh. "Tall, good-lookin' kid. Clean-shaved. Would'a been ridin' a plain bay gelding."

The bartender scratched at his chin for a few moments while Teddy danced nervously, foot to foot, then asked, "Geldin', you say? A plain one, no white?"

Slocum nodded. "Plain bay. Name'a Rufus, I think."

"Hmmm. Well, I don't remember the horse's name exactly, but I 'member that boy and his bay gelding. Awful nice-lookin' horse, it was. He was so nice, matter of fact, that our town sheriff tried to buy him. No deal, though. Why, you would'a thought the horse was right straight outta the wrapper, the way that kid doted on him!"

Slocum, who'd been in here before and questioned this same man about somebody or other—Bronc Dugan, maybe?—had learned not to try and drag out the information. He was fairly sure the bartender's name was Gary something-or-other, though, and that he'd tell them plenty if just given enough time and patience, and so he kept kneeing and kicking Teddy every time the kid began to look too excited.

In fact, Teddy finally had enough and moved off, down the bar, to put away his third (by that time) beer.

When Gary had finished talking and pouring beers, Slocum had boiled the thing down to this: Jorge had, indeed, been through the "town" about three months back. He had stayed the night over at the then-standing livery, and taken off the next morning for the south. He also learned that a posse from Tucson had been there a few days later—which Gary held back telling him until the end—looking for Jorge.

Obviously, they hadn't found him or there wouldn't still be paper out.

After Slocum thanked him very kindly for the information, he asked, "Don't suppose there's anyplace to stay around here, is there? Last time I was through, I slept in the barn with my horse."

Gary shook his head. "Nope."

After a pause, Slocum said, "Well, nobody'd object if we was to make camp out on the street, would they?"

"Reckon they wouldn't make a fuss," Gary responded. "We cook breakfast, too," he added hopefully.

"Good!" Slocum said, and at last let go of the double eagle he'd been palming throughout the conversation. Gary grabbed it as quick as a goose on a bug. "Reckon we'll be around for mornin' vittles, too."

Slocum lit himself a ready-made and once again congratulated himself on buying two packs back in Phoenix. Quirlies were all right, but you couldn't beat a ready-made for taste. He thought he'd try to remember this brand, too. They were nice and smooth.

He drained his beer and turned his head. "Hey, Teddy?"

The boy was practically asleep on the rail. But he looked up and said, "What?"

"You awake? Let's go out and make us a camp, all right?"

"Camp? Where?"

"On the street. Where else?"

Teddy shrugged and followed him through the batwing doors, giving the bartender a sleepy wave on the way out.

They made camp—right in the middle of the street—heated up the chicken, and ate. Teddy, who was nodding off at the start, came full awake when he smelled that chicken heating up. He swallowed his down, almost without taking a breath. It tasted pretty good to Slocum, too, but his mind was on Jorge. It had been three months since his escape. Chances were that he was long gone, into Mexico. Slocum figured they could ride forever without finding him, unless somebody remembered that horse.

Slocum did, but then, he was a horseman. Most other folks didn't think about horses at all, except for when they wanted to get somewhere. But this one, this one was a *horse*!

Slocum had seen him once, about a year back, when he was in Tucson picking up Lonny Chambers. He couldn't remember Lonny's face, but he could remember every curve and line of that horse. Rufus, the mayor called him, and he was a genuine Thoroughbred, leggy and lean and fine-headed. Tall, too. Slocum had guessed him at a bit over sixteen hands. Sixteen-one, maybe. He'd never seen a finer head on a horse. He remembered that it had a slight dish to it, with wide-set eyes and small ears, tipped in toward the center of his head, and a fine, small muzzle. He didn't look like he could herd cattle for shit, but you could tell he was bred to do something!

Slocum said, "Jump hedges," under his breath.

Teddy, who was on the apple pie by that time, said, "Huh?"

"What?" Slocum said before he realized he'd spoken out loud. "Oh, nothin'. Just thinkin' about the mayor's horse."

"Huh?" Teddy tipped his head quizzically.

"The one Jorge stole."

"Oh." The kid bought it, and didn't say another word. Good.

Slocum had counted on Jorge taking refuge right there in town, but now he realized how stupid that had been. Of course he'd go to Mexico! It was his homeland and U.S. marshals weren't allowed to cross the border. So they'd just put out paper when his tracks led them to it, and let it go. Bye-bye, Jorge. Bye-bye, Rufus. Bye-bye, reward. He didn't figure he wanted to take another trip down into Mexico.

Teddy might have a different opinion, but Teddy had to go where Slocum went.

And that was the end of it.

He didn't say as much to Teddy, though. Not this night. If they were going to argue, Slocum thought it had better wait until morning. A contented Teddy wouldn't take off for the southern hills in the dark, hard center of the night, and the last thing Slocum needed, besides Teddy gone missing again, was Teddy gone to Mexico.

The next morning, they took breakfast (which turned out to be passable) at the saloon, then rode out. Going north again, despite Teddy's protests.

"What in the devil you doin'?" he shouted at Slocum once they got clear of town. "This's the exact opposite way we should go!"

"Shut up," Slocum said, grabbing Teddy's reins. "Jorge's gone to Mexico, and we ain't ridin' all the hell over another country just for a couple grand. Or mayhap nothin'."

"Nothin'?"

"We don't know how good Jorge is at findin' himself places to hole up. And I ain't gonna waste my time goin' through every bear cave, cougar haunt, and jungle ruin in Mexico. No, here's our new quarry." Slocum let go of Teddy's reins long enough to dig a folded poster out of his pocket. He handed it to Teddy.

Teddy squinted at it.

Slocum knew exactly what he was reading. He'd pretty much memorized it last night. "Jonas Hendricks," the poster read, "Wanted for Murder and Thievery." Below that was a highly stylized drawing of Jonas, who looked like a mother killer and a baby splitter, all right. He was purported to be a midsized feller, with dirty blond hair and brown eyes and a ragged mustache. He was about five-foot-ten, around 170 pounds, and he'd half-killed a rancher up by Strawberry, and all-the-way killed a deputy sheriff that was in the posse that chased him up into the Bradshaws before they lost him.

The poster didn't say he was wanted for rustling, but given that he'd shot a rancher, Slocum was willing to put money on it. He was wanted dead or alive, too. That ought to please Teddy.

It did, by the looks of him. He was grinning by the time he finished reading. "Dead or alive," he said, handing the poster back to Slocum. "Now, that's a whole different kettle'a fish! And he was headed for the Bradshaws only two weeks back! Hell, we could be practically standin' on him right this second!"

Slocum tucked the poster away. "Thought that might be your reaction."

"And two grand's nothin' to sneeze at neither," a grinning Teddy replied. "Hot diggedy damn!"

Slocum chuckled. "Slow down, kid, slow down. We ain't got him yet." He, himself, was happy, but more relieved than anything else.

"He's about my size, too. I can beat anybody my size at wrastlin'!"

"He's also forty-three years old."

Teddy laughed. "Then I won't have to wrastle him. I'll jus' tip over his wheelchair!"

Slocum didn't answer. Shaking his head, he rode up front.

And not for the first time, he marveled that the kid had lived long enough to see twenty-four years.

13

They didn't find Jonas on that day, or on the next, but on the following day, Slocum picked up his trail. They had spent the last couple of days fanning out wide and back and forth, looking for signs of anyone's passing, finding nothing. But this morning, at about ten, Slocum spotted a break in the brush. Likely, it was just where some critter or other had spent the night—that had been the case several times before—so he rode toward it without alerting Teddy.

When he got there, the place wasn't clearly animal, though. In fact, he'd be damned if he ever heard of a bear or a coyote building a little fire, let alone trying to cover its remains with kicked-over grass and twigs.

He looked to the north, and shouted, "Teddy!" waving his hands.

When the kid finally heard him, Slocum signaled him to come over and come fast, which Teddy did. Together, they combed through the site.

Teddy found a pocket comb down in the weeds, and

Slocum found where Jonas had tied out his mare. There was fresh manure, full of processed corn and oats as well as the grasses that grew around here. Slocum figured it was made this morning. Still looked—and smelled—fresh anyhow.

The man might have killed a person, but at least he fed his horse right.

Teddy was ready to spring into action right that minute. He jumped on his mare, saying, "Hurry up! Hurry up, before he gets away!"

But Slocum took his time having a last look around the little campsite, then mounting up on Ace. "Take it easy, Ted. You even got an eye on the trail?"

"Huh?"

"You even know which way he went?"

Teddy took a deep breath before he said, "Well . . . up that way, I reckon." He pointed to the northwest, where the hills turned into mountains.

Slocum shook his head. "If you knew you'd killed somebody, plus stole a bunch'a cattle, but you also knew that you'd shaken off the posse, would you go up in the Bradshaws of your own free will?"

"Well, I . . ."

"No, you wouldn't. You'd go down toward the flat lands, which is exactly what Jonas did." Slocum stopped talking long enough to light a ready-made—and long enough for Teddy to think over what he'd said.

Teddy said, "Oh. I getcha," at about the same time Slocum shook out his sulfur tip.

He didn't figure that Teddy "got" it at all. In fact, he doubted Teddy had seen Jonas's trail, heading to the southwest. But he said, "C'mon," anyway, and started following it at a jog.

Gradually, Teddy figured it out. He began to see the little bends in the grasses, the place where a hoof had scuffed a patch of the loose topsoil. Well, what passed for topsoil out here anyway. He began to make out the trail, which, to Slocum, stood out like a red line painted over the scrub.

When they stopped, a couple of hours later, to rest the horses and grab some lunch, Teddy shook his head and said, "You're good. I mean it."

Slocum was making a couple of cheese sandwiches. "Not that good," he said. "Just practiced."

"Should I get a fire goin'?"

"No, Teddy. We'll have to make do with water. Not gonna be here that long." Slocum handed him a cheese sandwich, then finished making one for himself.

"Druther have coffee . . ." Slocum heard him mutter, but acted like he didn't hear. He'd rather have had coffee, too, but he didn't want the smoke of a fire alerting Jonas Hendricks. He figured Jonas couldn't be more than five miles ahead of them at this point.

Slocum ate his cheese sandwich fast, and washed it down with canteen water, as did Teddy. He noticed that the kid was already scouting the trail before them. Good. He was learning. Teddy hadn't mentioned any more remembering, and Slocum was hoping like hell that he never would. Or that if he did, he'd have the common sense to keep it to himself. He'd been granted a chance unheard of in the Territory, or anyplace else, so far as Slocum was concerned.

He'd best keep his mouth—and brain—closed.

Besides, Slocum liked him.

Teddy was a fast learner even if he was a tad impatient, and he had a fair sense for things. That'd improve as time went on and he learned more. And you sure couldn't beat his enthusiasm.

The moment Teddy finished eating, he stood up, walked back behind a cluster of palo verde, and took a long piss. And then he was on his horse again, ready to go.

"You wanna wait for me?" Slocum asked. He was behind the cactus now, emptying his own bladder.

"Well . . . sure! But can you hurry it up some?"

Slocum laughed while he buttoned up his pants. "Jesus, Teddy! Don't believe I've ever seen you so blasted eager! You gotta pay more attention to what you're doin' and what's goin' on around you. For instance," Slocum went on as he stepped out into the clear and swung up onto Ace, "just how many places could Jonas be hidin' right now, with your curly head in his sites?"

Teddy quickly swiveled his head, searching the distance with a surprised look on his face.

Slocum just shook his head, watching him. "Take it easy, Teddy," he said at last. "He ain't around. I checked this place good before I called a halt. But we're both gonna have to start watchin', lest we give him a chance to gun us both right outta the saddle. All right?"

Teddy said, "Slocum, I ain't never gonna learn all this stuff! Each time I think I got it licked, there's ten new things that come poppin' up!"

"Relax. You're pickin' it up good and fast. Just don't go gettin' cocky. 'Cocky' has got more men killed than guns and sabers put together, I'll bet."

Teddy brightened. "For real? You figure I'm pickin' it up fast?"

Slocum nodded. "Right good and fast. But you still got a lot to learn. One'a which is that your life could come to a screechin' halt at any given moment. And I mean *any* moment. While you're trackin' a man or haulin' him in, while you're pleasurin' yourself with a whore, while you're stopped on the trail to take a piss or have a coffee, anytime. You gotta learn people," he went on. "You may be thinkin' that the man you're hunting is just an outlaw, but you gotta keep the human in him, always. He's got hopes and fears, same as you. He's also got plans and schemes, like you, to make his life better. He's gotta eat and drink and shit and sleep, just like you do."

Teddy nodded, taking it all in like a little sponge. "Yessir," he said.

Slocum was surprised. It had been a few years since anybody had "sirred" him, and for just a second, he was pleased with himself. Just for one second, though. "Let's get goin'," he said, and clucked to Ace. "Same deal as before."

Which meant that Slocum rode to the right of the trail and Teddy kept to the left, each constantly scouting his side, and the center as well.

"Move into a slow lope," Slocum said. "Don't wanna spend a whole nother day trackin' this bastard."

Grinning again, Teddy complied, although he had to slow up some to keep pace with Slocum. To him, "a slow lope" meant just that.

Still, there was no sign of Jonas Hendricks except for his passage—a faint line in the weedy, brushy hills they'd traveled through today.

At about four, Slocum slowed them down. They'd been jogging, and Teddy, for one, was relieved. His mare had a jarring jog, and his butt was saddle-sore. "Why we slowin' down?" he called over the ten feet between him and Slocum.

"Hush!" Slocum snarled, and Teddy, taken aback, immediately shut his mouth. But what was going on? He hadn't spotted any change in the trail. He hadn't seen anything! In fact, he didn't know how anybody could. The weeds were so high that they grew higher than his head on horseback, for crying out loud.

But he sat there silently and waited.

He could barely make out Slocum's mounted figure through the ten thin feet of stems between them, until Slocum moved his horse over near him.

"What is it?" Teddy whispered.

"Listen."

"I been listenin' and I ain't heard diddly—"

"Hush!" Slocum pointed ahead.

Teddy listened. Nothing. He really concentrated, closing his eyes and straining to hear.

And there it was: Somebody, somewhere up ahead, was hammering something into the ground. He turned toward Slocum. "Tie-out stake?"

Slocum gave him a quick nod. "Probably."

Teddy kept his voice low, like Slocum. "How the hell'd you hear that while we was movin'?"

"Didn't," the big man replied. "Heard him talkin' to his horse."

When Teddy tilted his head quizzically, Slocum added, "He were't keepin' his voice down, or anythin'. Didn't know we was here. And still don't, if you hold your voice down to a roar."

Teddy couldn't see himself, but felt color rising up his neck and into his cheeks. He felt the way he had when his pa scolded him for doing something wrong, back when he was a little kid. He half expected a hand swat.

But it didn't come. Slocum signaled to him to follow, and began to slowly move forward, right over the top of Jonas's trail. The weeds were already beaten down from his prior passage.

Teddy was now behind, but at least he could see Slocum

clearly. And the horses sure made less clatter and commotion than they had while they were beating down the weeds.

Slocum twisted round in his saddle. "Follow my lead," he hissed, then turned forward again. It took Teddy a couple seconds to figure out what he meant, but now he knew— Slocum, before him, was riding out into the clear, and immediately Teddy was, too. The weeds had stopped, just like that.

He looked down, and saw that the earth under his horse's hooves was gone, too, changed abruptly to a shelf of yellow limestone, and that he heard the rush of water nearby. Slocum had moved along ahead of him when he saw Slocum lift an arm, wave, and shout, "Hello the camp!"

They were to go in as friends, then. It was a good idea. If Jonas had heard them talking before, he'd be a lot less likely to shoot first and ask questions later if they just rode into his camp, all friendly-like.

So, fine. Teddy put on his smiling face.

Just in time, too. Following Slocum, he rode out into a small clearing, bordered on one side by the tall grasses behind him, and bordered on the other by, first, a creek, and then, an abrupt rise.

In the center of the clearing, building himself a fire on the stone floor, sat Jonas Hendricks. His horse was off to the left, Teddy noted, staked out at the edge of the tall grass, which he was busily eating.

Slocum asked, "Mind if we climb down? It's been a long day!"

And Jonas answered, "Be obliged if you was to pull up some ground, fellers. Could use some company myself."

"We got vittles to share, if you're of a mind," Slocum said, "and Teddy, here? He makes the best coffee west of the Mississippi!"

Jonas finished building the fire, and while Teddy set the coffee to brew, Jonas asked Slocum, "What brings you fellers out here anyhow?"

Without a pause, Slocum replied, "You know Ol' Zeb Creed, don't you?"

Jonas shook his head. "Don't recall the name."

"Well, ain't surprised, I guess," Slocum said, nodding. "He ain't been out here for but three, mayhap four years. He owns the Circle Z. We're out looking for strays. Anyhow, I'm hopin' it's strays and not some low-life cattle rustler."

Slocum finished, and paused to take a long spit over toward the weeds. He slapped at his pockets before producing half a pack of ready-mades, which he held toward Jonas. "Care for a smoke?"

"No thanks," Jonas said. "Got my own. Tried those ready-mades, but I'd ruther have a hand-rolled anytime. No offense meant."

"None taken," Slocum said with a laugh. "Just means more for me." He pulled one out and lit it before he held the pack toward Teddy, who shook his head and mumbled, "No thanks." He wished Slocum'd *do* something, damn it! Was he gonna just sit and *chat* with this Jonas person until after dark?

14

Dinner had been cooked and eaten when Slocum brought out his ready-mades again. Lighting one, then shaking out the match, he accepted a fresh cup of coffee from Teddy (who looked increasingly nervous). He leaned forward, toward Jonas, who was seated across the fire from him.

Now, they had exchanged names earlier—Teddy and Jonas and John—but Slocum had given only his first name, since John could be John anyone, but "Slocum" was a name recognized by anybody with a price on his head, and quite a few others.

And Slocum said, "Jonas? Want to talk to you about somethin'."

"Sure."

"Now, about this rustlin' business, I—"

In a flash, Jonas was on his feet and drew his gun, but not as fast as Slocum. He'd snuck a Colt out about half an hour past, and he was ready.

"Just calm down, Jonas," Slocum soothed. "I know the

105

Territory's got paper out on you, but I'm thinkin' you didn't do it. Calm yourself and pull up some limestone, and let's talk 't over."

Warily, Jonas said, "I'll holster mine if you'll do the same."

"Done," said Slocum, and slid the Colt back into its holster.

Slowly, Jonas did the same and sat back down. He sat there in silence for a moment—while Slocum slid a glance over to make sure Teddy hadn't drawn—and then he said, "I didn't do it. It's that damn McAlister! He caught me while I was ridin' across his ranch, accused me of stealin'. I never stole a goddamn thing in my whole life, pinky swear! And if I was gonna steal somethin', it wouldn't have been anythin' of his. He hated me from the first time he set an eye on me. Hated my daddy, too, God rest his soul. That was all over water, least that's what started it. He finally run us outta business, but he held a grudge. Been more'n fifteen years, and I swear, that grudge'a his only got bigger."

Jonas paused to take a long drink of coffee. While he was at it, Teddy signaled something to Slocum, but Slocum waved him off. He wanted to hear the rest of Jonas's side.

"Anyhow, he must'a had a bug up his butt that day, because not five minutes later, the old bastard drew on me! Right on the middle of a cow pasture, sitting big as life on that pinto horse'a his, he drew on me!" Jonas shook his head wearily and sighed.

"How'd you come to kill him, then? I mean, if he had the drop on you?"

Jonas's forehead wrinkled right up. "Kill him? I sure didn't kill him. Might'a knocked him off that old pinto, but I didn't kill him. See, his foreman come over the crest of the hill about then, and while his head was turned, I freed up my leg from the stirrup and gave him a kick. He went down off that horse like a beaver off a log, and I set my spurs to my horse. And that was it."

Slocum rolled this over in his head before he asked, "You didn't hear any shots while you were high-tailin' it?"

"Not till I got myself pretty far away. At least over the crest of the next hill. There was two shots, so I figured they was both chasin' me. So I kicked ol' Sunny and let him go. Never left a place so fast in all my borned days! Got myself clear up, almost into the Bradshaws, when I seen that it wasn't just ol' McAlister and his foreman. They'd put a whole damn posse together and was headed for me, goin' full tilt and shootin' to beat the band."

Teddy, who had been silent up to this point, asked, "You shoot at 'em then?"

Jonas said, "Well, it didn't look like they was gonna give me even a part of a chance, so once me and Sunny—that's my horse—got goin' again, I started shootin' back. Emptied my damn gun. But they just kept comin'. We clumb and we clumb, and then I had to get off and lead him, and then—finally—we got to a place where the trail, such as it was, dead-ended in a drop-off cliff, down to the river. I didn't have no choice, and ol' Sunny seemed to know that. 'Cause when I whacked him across the butt, he jumped down into that river, and I went in next."

Slocum was pretty damn impressed, and nodded his head in appreciation. "Helluva story, Jonas. One helluva tale."

"And then what happened?" Teddy broke in eagerly. "I mean, you and your horse, you made it out. But what then? Did the posse jus' give up? Why'd you decide to ride down outta the Bradshaws? Did the—?"

Slocum lifted his hand, silencing the boy. He was going to have to learn some self-control sooner or later, and Slocum hoped it'd be sooner.

"I figger Jonas has about worn himself out with the tellin' of it," he said. "If there's more, he can tell you tomorrow, okay?"

Jonas sent Slocum a grateful nod.

But Slocum himself didn't stop. He said, "Just one more thing, Jonas."

"Reckon I can handle it."

"Who's the heir to everythin'? I mean, who gets McAlister's cows and land and stuff?"

Jonas shrugged. "His daughter and son-in-law, I reckon. Who killed him?"

"They live around here? I mean, in the Territory?" Slocum asked, ignoring the question about McAlister's fate.

"Well, sure they do," Jonas replied as if Slocum was an idiot. "Be awful hard to ramrod a ranch from a whole different Territory!"

Slocum was beginning to see the light. "So his son-in-law was his foreman?"

"Well, sure," Jonas said. Then, "Sorry. I leave that part out?"

"Yup," said Slocum while he dug out another ready-made. "It makes a difference, y'know."

Even Teddy was beginning to get it now. He shoved back his hat and took a scratch at his forehead, saying, "I'll be diddly-damned."

"Why don't we all get some rest?" said Slocum. He lit his ready-made and shook out the match. "I'll take first watch."

Teddy looked like he was halfway asleep already, but he started to argue.

"Teddy, just go the hell to sleep, okay? I'll wake you when it's your turn."

"Yessir," the kid muttered, and lay right down, pulling his thin blanket over himself.

"How 'bout me?" asked Jonas, who apparently didn't

realize he was under arrest. Slocum decided to wait till the morning to tell him. Let him have a peaceful night's sleep.

"You're too tuckered out to still be talkin'," Slocum said, and took a drag off his ready-made. "You get yourself some shut-eye, too."

"Well, you wake me when you want relief," Jonas said. "I don't mind tellin' you that I ain't had a good restful night's sleep since this crap happened to me."

Slocum nodded. Teddy was already snoring softly. Slocum said, "Don't blame you one bit. Go on, get yourself some shut-eye, Jonas."

Slocum waved him down, and that was that. He sat guard himself, occasionally dozing, the whole night through.

It was morning, and the sun was bright. They'd already had breakfast, put out the fire, and seen to the horses. And Slocum still hadn't told Jonas that he was under arrest. Truth be told, he liked the fellow as well as believed his story. He was hoping that Pete, back in Phoenix, would see it the same way. But first, he had to tell Jonas, who, at present, was snugging up the girth on his horse.

"Jonas?" said Slocum. "Like to talk to you for a second."

Jonas finished off the girth and turned around. "Sure," he said, smiling. "What's on your mind, John?"

Oops. Slocum figured he'd best tell him his name while he was at it.

He said, "Sit down, Jonas," as he perched himself on a rock. "I've got some hard news for you."

Jonas, his brow working, sat on a boulder opposite Slocum's. "What is it? We been surrounded durin' the night?" He shot a glance left, then right.

Slocum shook his head. "No, Jonas. Ain't nobody out there. They're in here."

Jonas's brows knotted. "Huh?"

"Jonas, I believe you, I truly do. But when a man has a price on his head, it's my job to bring him in. You know, get things sorted out proper."

"I thought you worked for ol' man Creed."

"Sorry I had to go and fib a little. Ain't no Zeb Creed. Made him up. And I also didn't tell you my whole name. It's Slocum. John Slocum."

Jonas's eyes grew so large Slocum thought they'd pop from his head. "S-S-Slocum?" he stuttered. "*The* Slocum? The bounty hunter?" Suddenly he looked terrified.

Slocum thumped Jonas's leg with the outside of a fist. "Don't take it so hard, Jonas. Between the two of us, I'm thinkin' that marshal down to Phoenix is gonna believe your story, too. Pete's a fair man. Sounds to me like the old man's son-in-law was in a mite too much hurry to inherit."

Jonas looked shocked, but no words came out. Then he sputtered, "You gotta take me in? *To Phoenix?*"

"It's better than lettin' you go. Territory's got a poster out on you for murder and theft, and it's posted for dead or alive. You think you'd have a chance out there on your own?" Slocum paused, then added, "Best thing to do is to clear your name. Makes things a whole lot easier in the long run."

Slowly, Jonas nodded. "In the short run, too, I reckon. All right," he said with a sigh. "I'll go in with you. Best to get this thing cleared up. I reckon what you're sayin' is right on the money."

Slocum stood up. "Good man, Jonas."

Jonas stood up, too. "I hope so, Slocum. And I hope to hell you're right."

Me, too, Slocum thought. *Me, too.*

The three men found their way out of the tall grasses and back through the foothills, and soon were on their way down to Phoenix. Jonas wore no chains or ropes, he just rode along, keeping pace, from time to time shaking his head and muttering. Just what he was muttering, Slocum didn't understand, but it sounded woeful.

"Dasn't you think we should tie him up or somethin'?" Teddy asked one night when they camped. His eyes had been trained on Jonas's hands right through the day's ride, and the day before, and the day before.

It wasn't that Teddy didn't trust Jonas, Slocum thought. Well, all right, Teddy just plain didn't trust much of anybody.

"Nope," said Slocum. "He's fine as is." Jonas was off collecting fuel for the fire, which wasn't an easy task when you were most of the way down on the flat, which they were.

"You doin' any more'a that rememberin'?" Slocum asked.

Teddy twisted his head. "No. Why?"

"Just wonderin'," Slocum replied with a shrug. "That's all."

"Hello the camp!" Jonas's voice rang out. He was coming in with a load of combustibles for the fire.

Slocum waved. He called out, "Aha! Hello the bringer of fire!" and laughed.

Jonas looked a sight, all right. He had picked up every conceivable thing that would burn and strapped it all to his back, so that he looked like a medieval peasant.

When Teddy said, "I don't get it," Slocum laughed all the harder.

15

The next afternoon, Slocum, Teddy, and a dejected Jonas rode into Phoenix and went straight to the marshal's office. When Slocum led them into Pete's office, Pete looked up and said, "This feller don't look Mexican to me. Thought you were goin' after Jorge."

Slocum pulled out a chair and motioned the other men down, while saying, "That didn't work out so well. He's gone down into Mexico, sure as shootin'. Anyways, I would if I was him."

Pete nodded sagely. "Who's this?" He pointed at Jonas.

"Jonas Hendricks," Slocum replied, "though I wanna have a talk about him. Me and Teddy, we decided he's been framed."

Pete riffled through some papers on his desk. "Hm. Seems now you're wanted for two murders, Jonas. McAlister died of his wounds a few days back." He sighed, stood, and pulled out his keys. "Best you come along with me."

Teddy jerked to his feet, shouting, "No!"

But Slocum got him sat back down. "Things gotta go through channels, kid," he said. "Don't you worry." He looked over at Jonas, who was halfway out the door with Pete at his back. "You neither, Jonas."

Jonas nodded glumly and went on his way.

"But Jonas knows the story best!" Teddy complained. "He can tell it better'n us!"

"That he can, but they still gotta go through the formalities. And dollars to doughnuts, Pete'll send us back up to do some snoopin' for him."

Teddy cocked a brow. "He will?"

Slocum nodded. "Wait and see."

They spent the night at Katie's, and she was past thrilled to see Slocum again so soon.

"Word's got around that I'm sleepin' with a customer," she said late that night after Slocum'd had her twice and was sitting by the window, smoking a ready-made. "I keep sayin' that you're not no customer, that you're special, but I guess folks figure that if I'm sleepin' with anybody, that means I'm open for business."

Slocum nearly dropped an ash on his bare leg. "Anybody in particular givin' you a hard time?"

She smiled. "Other than you, you mean?"

"Now, Katie . . ."

"Sorry, couldn't help myself," she said. "But yes. Bert Gimble—he owns the bank—he's been sniffin' around somethin' fierce. And Lance Breakenridge practically raped me when I was walking home from the market on Tuesday. Said he'd heard I was givin' it up to somebody, and wasn't he just as good? And I said to take his business someplace else, 'cause I wouldn't ever sleep with the likes of him, all stinkin' of cattle."

"I smell like cattle half the time," Slocum said, smiling.

"Well, on you it's like man perfume. On him, it's like he just rolled in a manure pile."

Slocum laughed and motioned her over. She stood up, stark naked, and crossed the room to curl into his lap.

He said, "You were tellin' me how he almost raped you. What stopped him?"

"Me. Hollerin' at the top'a my lungs. Four of the gals come runnin' and started whackin' him with umbrellas and walkin' sticks, whatever they grabbed outta the front hall. And boy, he sure took off in a big hurry. Doubt he'll be botherin' me again, least in this neighborhood."

Slocum had taken her breast into his hand and begun to suckle her, but he broke it off long enough to chuckle and say, "Bet he won't. But you gotta be careful. You're still a mighty beautiful woman, Katie. You gotta watch out for those sonsabitches."

"I do," she said. "Now get back to business."

He did, sliding his fingers between her legs and taking her nipple into his mouth again, and he kept on rubbing her and tickling that special spot between her legs, and suckling at her bosom until she came, gasping and writhing in his lap.

And that was just the beginning of it.

At roughly dawn, Slocum was awakened by a pounding on the door. Telling Katie to stay put, he got out of bed and wrapped himself in a sheet. He opened the door to find a nervous Teddy, already dressed and ready to ride.

"C'mon, Slocum!" he urged. "We gotta ride north today! This morning!"

Slocum let out a long breath, then said, "Okay, Teddy. Can you wait till I get dressed?"

"Yeah, sure. Thanks." And he popped down the hall again, just like that.

From behind him came Katie's sweet voice. "You have to go, baby?"

Without turning around, he said, "'Fraid so, Katie darlin'," and softly closed the door.

He didn't hear anything else out of her except, "Well, shit."

He was dressed and downstairs in about five minutes, startling Teddy, who was coiled in the arms of Sally, the little redhead he'd taken up with the first time Slocum brought him to Katie's. The only one since, Slocum realized. Was Teddy getting himself into something serious?

Of course, it couldn't hurt, Slocum thought. Teddy'd have plenty of cash when they came out of this. Enough to buy a new house in town. Enough to cover him for a few years. Maybe marriage would settle him down permanently. Maybe he'd never remember.

"Teddy?" he said, and the boy turned around so fast that he nearly knocked himself—and Sally—over.

"Easy, boy," he said with a smile. "I'm gonna grab some grub first."

"Okay," said Teddy, and eased himself back into Sally's arms.

Slocum went to the kitchen, where he found Iris and another girl, May, having breakfast. "Mind if I join you gals?" he asked while he pulled up a chair.

"Seems to me you're already sat," Iris answered, grinning. "Breakfast?"

"You got my number, all right."

She stood up and went over to the stove, pulling down a plate from the shelves in the process. "What'll you have?"

"What you got? No, wait. Don't list it out. Just gimme some of everythin'." After last night with Katie, he was hungry as a bear!

Iris scooped up something from every pot and skillet,

then set the plate down in front of him. "Coffee, too?" she asked.

"You betcha." Before him, on the plate, rested the breakfast of his dreams. Sausage, ham, bacon, eggs, hash browns, cottage fries, and two pancakes on the side, dripping with butter and syrup.

There may have been more, but if it there was, it was hidden beneath something else. He dug into the pancakes straight away, then the sausage, then the eggs. He was most of the way though the bacon and heading for the hash browns when Katie made an appearance. She looked awful pretty this morning—a sight better than he did, that was for sure. She had slipped on a soft blue dress, low-cut but still fairly prim, and pulled her long russet hair up into a knot at the top of her head.

She looked downright beautiful.

Slocum dropped his fork and said, "My gosh, Katie! You surely do look a picture!"

"Why, thank you, Mr. Slocum," she replied, then curtsied. "Is the meal to your satisfaction?" she asked primly.

"Now, Miss Katie, I'd like to talk to you about these hash browns," Slocum began. He scooted his chair back from the table, turning slightly. "Please take a seat." He held out his arm.

She took it, and sat in his lap.

"There," he said. "That's fine." He picked up the fork again and cut off a bite of hash browns. "Open wide," he said, bringing the fork up to her mouth.

She obliged and took in the potatoes, although she whispered, "This is a little different than the last time I was in this position . . ."

"Didn't your mama teach you to chew with your mouth closed?" Slocum teased.

She elbowed him in the ribs.

"Slocum?" Teddy shouted from the other room. "Are we goin' or ain't we?"

"Sorry, baby," Slocum said. "Duty calls."

She eased herself up off his lap, purposely wiggling her backside in his face, then sat down beside him, in the next chair over.

"Slocum?" Teddy called again. "You comin'?"

Slocum slowly stood up, grabbing the ham slice in one hand and the rest of the bacon and sausages in the other. "Too good to leave behind," he said sheepishly.

"You'd best leave before that boy busts a vocal cord," she said.

"See you when I get done, hon," he said. He'd explained their new assignment last night.

She said, "I'll be here waiting, darlin'."

They rode north, up toward McAlister's ranch, which was just this side of Prescott. The trip itself wasn't bad. Just green, rolling hills, cactus, and the occasional upthrust of rock, as if the land were practicing for the mountains to come. Slocum knew that when they started to see trees, they'd be almost there. That'd take them another day, he guessed, but the way Teddy was acting, you'd think they'd get there today and have the whole mess wrapped up by nightfall.

The bloody little eager beaver.

Slocum was in no such hurry. He knew that once they got there, it'd take a good while before they "noodled" out the right kind of information from the locals. Mainly because folks didn't just open up to a stranger. It'd take a bit to gain their trust. He couldn't wait to tell Teddy that he was gonna have to take a job at the hardware or the general store! He could just see it now: Teddy Cutler, from wanted man to whitewash salesman in a month.

Smirking to himself, Slocum rode along in silence.

* * *

When they finally came to a town—Squash Blossom was its name—Slocum rode into a place he'd never been before, although he'd sure seen towns like it. It was small, with one main street, dotted with wooden buildings. There was a mercantile that doubled as a dry goods store, a tiny livery with a board-fenced paddock attached to one side, a sheriff's office and a city hall, a café, a saloon, and a blacksmith's. That last one was over by the livery, too, and the city hall wasn't much bigger than what you could fit a few offices in.

The mayor's, he figured. He didn't know who else, in such a small place. But they did have a railroad line going through. That was likely there to mostly service the cattle ranches so they could ship their beef to market. He doubted they had much passenger traffic.

They tied their horses to the rail in front of the saloon, and swearing Teddy to silence, Slocum led the way inside.

There wasn't much going on, by the looks of things. Oh, there were a few men at the bar, three more playing poker at a table, but that was it, except for the bartender. He looked accessible enough, though. Slocum decided to try him first.

They moseyed on over to the bar—which at least was a real bar, not a plank held up with barrels—and ordered a couple of beers.

"Why'd you pick here for first?" Teddy whispered.

"You always pick the saloon first," Slocum whispered back. "Like with ladies, you always go to the hairdresser's or the seamstress's first. You go to the place where folks meet to gossip."

The barkeep brought the beers, offered them a sandwich if they wanted one—they said no—and then was off to the other end of the bar to polish glasses and gossip with the fellows standing at that end.

Slocum leaned back against the bar, bringing his beer with him, and casually studied the crowd. Cowhands, mostly, except for the men over at the poker table. One of them looked like a recent train passenger—a card sharp, if Slocum was any guess. He reckoned he'd learn the most over there right now. The barkeep was too busy, chatting with his buddies.

"Are you decent at poker?" he asked Teddy.

"Sure. I'm whiz-bang!"

Slocum puffed out a little sigh. "I mean, really. There's a sharp sittin' over at that table, and I ain't stakin' you to no million dollars."

Teddy's eyes went down to the floor. "Guess I'm not up to playin' with no card sharp. You goin'?"

Slocum said, "I aim to." And just like that, he was walking across the room, beer in hand. He figured they had only three players, and a fourth would make them real happy. Fresh money, and all.

When he got to the table, he put his hand on the back of the empty chair. "This a private game, or can anybody play?"

16

"Have a seat, friend," the sharp said.

And the other two echoed his invitation, although a little belatedly. The taller of the two said, "You just travelin' through town, mister?"

"Name's John," Slocum said, "and I'm lookin' for work. Generally don't stop, but I need a little tidin' over."

The shorter one said, "Howdy, John. I'm Shorty, Shorty Simpson. This here," he said, nodding toward the taller man, "is my brother. We call him Hawk."

Hawk smiled and retorted, "If you heard the half of it, you'd pick Hawk, too. Same deal for Shorty."

Shorty grinned and asked, "Whose deal is it?"

"Your brother's," said the sharp, then introduced himself to Slocum. "Hello, John. Glad to have you in the game. I am Wendell Howard. Call me Dell."

Slocum nodded while Hawk shuffled. "Glad to meet all'a you. Glad to see some cards, too. Haven't played since I left Phoenix."

121

"Aw, that ain't so far," said Hawk, dealing the cards. "Couple'a days, if you know the right paths to take. Straight five-card draw, nothin' wild, two-bit limit."

Dell, across the table from Slocum, looked annoyed, but didn't say anything. Slocum figured he should have known what to expect when he saw the town. But then, maybe he was running dry, too, as Slocum claimed that he was. Maybe it was just a stop-off for a little pocket cash.

Hawk finished dealing, and they began to play. The first hand went to Shorty. It was Slocum's turn to deal next, and Shorty won that hand again. Then Shorty dealt and Hawk won.

While they were playing, Slocum learned that both Hawk and Shorty rode for the same outfit, the Double A. Slocum also learned that it was McAlister's old outfit, the only one in the nearby vicinity, and that they were looking for hands, on account of it was time to break horses.

Slocum jumped on that like a duck on a June bug. "What's McAlister pay?" he asked, although he was well aware that the old man was dead.

"Dollar a day and found," replied Hawk. "'Course it ain't McAlister's place no more." He bowed his head. "He passed away last Saturday. Gut shot by some goddamn cattle rustler!"

Hawk held back his tears, but Shorty couldn't. A lot of sniffling and snuffling started coming from his side of the table. Slocum didn't look at him. The man deserved some privacy. But to Hawk, he said, "You got *rustlers* around here?"

"Accordin' to the new boss, we do." Hawk appeared not to be in his camp.

"Who's the new boss?"

"McAlister's son-in-law," Hawk replied. "Heber Johnson." Slocum cocked a brow. "He Mormon?"

Hawk shook his head. "I guess his folks was, though. He don't claim to be anythin'. Married the boss's daughter, though. Dora. Awful nice gal to get mixed up with trash like that."

"Hawk!" Shorty hissed sharply. "Don't go talkin' about our employer that'a way!"

"It's the truth, Shorty. A pig's ear don't get changed into a silk purse on account'a who he weds or who he works for. Or what he owns."

Shorty just sat there, sniffing. "Not cryin' for him," Shorty mumbled. "For McAlister."

"Then go right ahead. He was a pig-headed old fool, but he paid good and fair."

Slocum butted in, "Why you sayin' he was pig-headed, Hawk?"

"Just certain ways. Not all'a the time. Like that water rights thing he had goin' on for years 'n years with the Hendrickses. That was just plain stupid. We got plenty of water, and so did Hendricks. McAlister just wanted it all for himself, and that was that. It was Hendricks's boy—a middle-aged man by now—who supposedly shot him. He was rustlin' cows out on the south range. McAlister found him and took a slug, then Heber come and chased Hendricks off. Accordin' to Heber anyhow." Hawk didn't look any too convinced.

Slocum found this information to be interesting and perhaps useful. "Like to ride out to the ranch with you or at least get directions. I'm a pretty fair hand at bustin' broncs."

"You sure?" Hawk arched a brow. "No offense, but breaking horses is generally a young man's game."

"Don't worry about me, none," Slocum said. "I can take care'a myself. By the way, who'd you say your foreman was?"

"Didn't. Was Heber, but now it's me."

Slocum laughed. "Been talkin' to the boss the whole time!"

Hawk just grinned. "So, you interested in that job?"

"I sure am. Oh, and the whole of my name's John Quincy," Slocum said off the top of his head. He figured he could remember it, on account of President Adams. "Should I keep on callin' you Hawk, now that you're my boss?"

"Probably wanna call him worse than that," said a smirking Shorty from the other side of the table.

And from beside him, the card sharp, Dell Howard, said, "*Now* can we play another game?"

Slocum laughed. "Sure. And I'm sure sorry, but I don't believe I seen you shuffle those cards, Dell. Mind?"

"Of course not," Dell replied, although he looked like he minded quite a bit. But he shuffled the cards a few times, shoved them over to Hawk to cut, which he did.

Resigned, Dell began to deal.

Slocum said, "Mind if I start tomorrow?"

"Not a problem," replied Hawk, intent on his cards.

"Gotta get my little brother settled in," Slocum said, tipping his head toward Teddy. "He ain't much for ranch work."

Shorty, who had at last stopped weeping, said, "I heard that old man Fowler's lookin' for somebody. Down to the hardware," he added by way of explanation.

"I thank you a lot," Slocum said, nodding. "I'll get him right down there, soon's I finish this hand!"

"What's your name?" Slocum asked for the hundredth time. Or it seemed so to him anyway.

"Ted Quincy," came the tired reply. Teddy was about to fall asleep in Slocum's armchair. "I'm from Alabama. I'm twenty-four. I don't much like ranch work."

"Where in Alabama?"

"Albany. And why I gotta say I'm from Alabama in the first place?" Teddy whined. "Can't I be from Phoenix? I at least *been* to Phoenix!"

"I know. But you can bet none'a them has been to Alabama."

Teddy sighed. "What about fightin' in the War? Surely some'a them was through there!"

"The War's nearly thirty years past, Teddy. And most'a the men round here just ignored it anyhow."

There was a long silence while Teddy thought. Then, at last, he said, "My name's Ted Quincy, I'm twenty-four, I'm not likin' ranch work for much'a nothin', and I'm from Albany, Alabama, on Windsong Creek, and you're my big brother, *John*."

He put a heavy emphasis on Slocum's first name.

Slocum said, "You keep that up, I'm gonna change your first name to Candy Ass."

"Sonofabitch," Teddy growled.

"There, that's better. That's more . . . brotherly."

"Bite me," Teddy said while he stood up.

Slocum was at least taking it with some humor, and he said, "Only if'n you're snake-bit, brother Ted."

Teddy didn't answer, just let himself out. *Just as well*, Slocum thought as the door softly closed. *He knows the drill anyhow.*

He wandered over and sat in the chair by the window, pulling his ready-mades from his pocket. After lighting one, he sifted through his pockets again to make certain he still had the directions out to the Double A spread.

He did. It ought to be easy to find.

He could just about hang Heber right now, but he'd had enough doings with the law to know that he needed hard evidence, not just say-so. And hard evidence was what he hoped to ferret out at the Double A.

And someone to testify to it.

That was going to be the hard part, he knew.

Puffing on his smoke, he stared out over the town. Well, what there was of it anyway.

Morning came, and when it did, Slocum and Teddy went over the café and grabbed some breakfast, then down the street to the mercantile, which had a side entrance marked HARDWARE. While Teddy nosed around, Slocum found Fowler, then signaled Teddy. "This here's my brother I been tellin' you about," said Slocum.

"Hello, Ted," said Mr. Fowler, a kind-faced man with gray hair and a goatee. "I understand you're lookin' for work."

Teddy took off his hat without being told and held it in front of him with both hands. "Yessir, I am, sir," he said. Slocum almost passed out. The kid actually had some manners!

Fowler looked Teddy up and down. "You have any experience in the retail field?"

"Yessir. When I was sixteen, I worked at our mercantile, and when I was eighteen, I worked at our gunsmith's shop. I can make change and handle customers and fix guns, too."

Slocum just shook his head. The kid was perfect. Perfect!

Fowler scratched at his chin. "Can you work for a dollar a day and a cot in the back room?"

All smiles, Teddy answered in the affirmative.

And Fowler said, "Hired."

Before Teddy got down to clerking, Slocum pulled him aside. "I'm goin' back to the hotel," he said. "Gimme your key and I'll pack you up and drop it off before I leave town, okay?"

Teddy handed over the key without a word except to answer Fowler's call. "Coming, sir!" he said with a sideways snarl to Slocum, and then he was gone.

17

The ride out to the Double A spread was easy and peaceful. Slocum enjoyed the ride. He was satisfied that Teddy was tucked away safely at the hardware—and his mare at the stable, with her board paid a month in advance—and he was actually looking forward to his new "job." Busting broncs wasn't exactly his forte, but if they let him do it his own way, he could break more horses than any of them.

Well, he used to be able to anyhow.

He hadn't had to break any horses—outside of his own, personal mounts—for years, so this was going to be a challenge. The best kind of challenge, though. He loved horses, and he loved seeing them trained without breaking their spirit. He just hoped Heber, the sonofabitch, would let him try.

He turned a long, looping corner in the tall weeds, and came out on a place where the grasses were short, and where the original owners had built up the first cabin on the site.

It had been expanded over the years, of course. Big additions, small additions, all combined to make a rather wandering but impressive Spanish-style hacienda. He saw a big holding barn at the far edge of the clearing, and a smaller barn—with a paddock and a round bullpen—for horses a little closer, and a bunkhouse. If there were more buildings, they were hidden behind these, because he sure couldn't see them.

There were a cluster of hands down by the corral—which was filled with horses, just off the range—and so he rode straight for it.

"Howdy!" he said at his most chipper. "Hawk around?"

One of the fellows shouted, "Hey, Hawk!" and sure enough, he came walking up.

"Howdy, John," he said. Then, "Fellers, this here is John Quincy. He's hirin' on to help us get through the horse breakin' time."

Slocum swung down, while several of the men came over to have a look at Ace, admiring his depth and legs and head. Slocum was proud of Ace, so he took the compliments well.

"What first, Hawk?" he asked.

"Well, let's get you settled first and get your horse put up, and then let's start you breakin' horses. C'mon." Hawk led him down to the bunkhouse, which was just, as Slocum discovered, a long, narrow building with cots running down each side. He followed Hawk to a bunk. Hawk said, "This one's free. Tex up and quit about a month back, so ain't nobody gonna fight you for it."

Slocum set down his saddlebags and bedroll and rifle, which Hawk greatly admired, hefting it this way and that. "She shoot straight?"

Slocum nodded. "Straight as I need anyhow."

"Might's well leave them guns in here, too. Don't like it when fellers are armed when there's horse breakin' to do.

We had a man killed last year, shot himself in the chest from gettin' tangled up with a wild mare."

Slocum nodded, and stripped off his gun belt and his cross-draw rig.

Hawk said, "Good. Now let's get your horse put up."

The horse barn had tic-in stalls, period. Usually, Slocum rented a box stall for his horse, but he'd just have to put up with it, he guessed. As he pulled the tack off Ace, he said softly, "Sorry, pal. You'll just have to wait for me to be done to get better lodgings."

Hawk showed him where they stored the tack, and then they walked back up to the men and horses.

"Best to take 'er easy at first," Hawk said, his sandy hair glinting in the sun when he took his hat off to wipe his brow.

"Got it," Slocum replied. He wasn't too wild about sitting on a bucking bronc first thing either. "Been a while for me. Best to ease back into it."

"Good," said Hawk. "Afraid you were gonna fight me."

Slocum smiled and shook his head.

They reached the men.

Hawk said, "Marv, cut out that bay mare. The one with the white star. Slocum's gonna give 'er a ride."

Marv stepped forward. He was a short hand with dark hair and darker eyes, and he looked scared.

"Go ahead, Marv, bring 'er out!" cried one of the others. A chuckle rippled through the crowd.

"You playin' with me?" Slocum asked Hawk. "She the toughest one in the bunch or somethin'?"

"Nope. It's just that Marv's afraid to go into the ketch pen." He turned toward the group. "Harry, give Marv a hand, okay?"

The one called Harry darted to the fence, near where the mare in question was standing, and threw a loop over her head. He worked her over to the fence deftly, then shouted, "Marv, get your ass over here!"

Marv still didn't move, so Slocum took off. "Where you want me?" he asked Harry.

"Over by the gate. Dang that Marv anyhow!"

Slocum went around to the gate, unlatched it, but held it closed. When Harry came close and the mare was on the other side of the gate, Slocum eased it open just far enough so that she could slide through. Which she did.

And then she began to buck, going for first one man, then the other. One of the other hands came running and finally got a second rope around her neck. Slocum took the rope, and they began to move her, slowly but surely, as she bucked and spun and hopped, toward the other corral.

They got her inside and roped to the snubbing post, then backed off. "You forget to halter break 'er, Hawk?" Slocum called.

The men laughed.

Slocum pulled the breaking saddle and blanket and bridle off the fence, then said, "Anybody got a halter on him?"

"What you got planned?" Hawk asked him. "We don't usually mess with halters on new stock."

"And you had a man killed last year," Slocum said. "Just gimme a little leeway on this one. I got a way that'll gentle her down without quite so much bumpin' and bruisin'."

Hawk held his hands wide. "I'm open to suggestions. Go on ahead. Marv, go get him a halter."

For once, Marv left the crowd and ran toward the barn. He came right back with a halter that looked like it would fit the mare, and handed it to Slocum, saying, "Here." Then he walked back into the crowd.

"Chatty sort, ain't he?" Slocum said softly as he tested the halter for strength, turning it over in his hands.

"Yeah," said Hawk, and Slocum left him to walk back to

the mare's pen. She was still snubbed tight to the post. He entered slowly.

When she saw him, she started striking out with her front hooves, then kicking out with her hind ones. "Tut tut, now, girl," he said in a soft singsong. "That ain't gonna do you a bit'a good, an' we both know it. Now, why don't you settle yourself down a bit, and you'll see what kind'a fun this can be, okay?"

She stopped lashing out and stood there, eyeing him and sweating to beat the band.

"Now see what you've gone and done?" he said in the same singsong. "You got yourself all hot and lathered up like there's been a cougar after you. I ain't no big cat, girl, no such thing. No, I'm the feller what's gonna get you all nice and tame, so you'll have good vittles all year round, and serve a purpose for one'a these fine fellers back there."

He was at her side now. She didn't move a muscle.

"That's a good girl, isn't it?" he soothed. "Good and quiet. Good and halter broke. I hope."

He checked the ropes. Nobody had thought to get a loop over her nose, but the ones around her neck were sure tight. He cupped her muzzle carefully, letting her get his scent— and letting her get a little more striking out of her system. And then he brought up the halter to let her smell it.

She didn't like it much—especially when he slipped it over her nose—but in the end, she accepted it. He began working at the ropes, talking: all the time, talking softly, mesmerizing her with his voice.

Most of the hands were up on the fence now, watching curiously, but with quiet admiration. Slocum was glad they appreciated it. Maybe that'd lead to more humane horse breakings in the future.

He tied the end of the long rope he freed up first to the lead ring on her halter, and then he moved back. She was free now, connected to him only by the rope on her halter. She made no attempt to kick or show him her teeth, although she appeared relieved to be free of the ropes.

"That's a good girl, good girl, good girl." He was running out of things to say, but he kept talking anyhow.

Slowly, he moved her away from the post and began to lunge her around the pen.

In town, Teddy was on his best behavior. He had just finished with his third customer—a farmer who bought several reels of barbed wire to keep the Double A's cattle out of his crops—and was happily entering the man's purchase in the faded brown leather book in which his boss recorded every single transaction when, lo and behold, his boss came over into the hardware side of the store.

"Teddy?"

"Yes, Mr. Fowler?"

"Been watchin' you."

"Yessir?"

"You're doin' a good job. Just thought you ought'a know that."

Teddy let out an unintentional grin. "Thanks, Mr. Fowler!"

"Think a man ought'a know when he's doing a good job, that's all. Now, you can take lunch right on the stroke of noon, but be back by twelve-thirty. If'n you'd like, my wife brings a lunch basket. You're welcome to it. Today, I think she's got meatloaf sandwiches."

"That's mighty kind'a you, Mr. Fowler. I'd like to do that." He knew lunch would cost him almost half a day's wage, and he also knew that Fowler was no more a fool than he was. He'd go along and do what was right and keep all his ducks in a row, like his mama used to say, until they found out whatever was needed to free Jonas.

He reckoned he'd know when it was time.

That was funny. He hadn't thought about his mama for a coon's age. Was she even still alive? That was something he ought to know. *What kind of a son doesn't even know if his mama's alive or not?* he thought, shaking his head.

Someone else came in, asking for paint for a young girl's bedroom. So they went on over to the paint shelves and began to look at the paint chips. Teddy forgot all about himself until a nice lavender was picked and paid for, along with a couple of brushes and some turpentine. He had to admit, he was surprised that a town this small even had lavender paint right there, and didn't have to order out to Kansas City or Chicago or somewhere.

Surprised and impressed.

And he told Mr. Fowler as much as they sat that noon, eating meatloaf sandwiches with pickles, and washing them down with the bucket of beer that Fowler had Teddy pick up at the saloon.

Teddy had to admit that he'd never enjoyed a meal more, even with Slocum. Mr. Fowler was a right soul, funny or serious, and several times Teddy felt the truth about himself and Slocum creeping onto his tongue, but stopped it in the nick of time. Mr. Fowler was somebody you just naturally wanted to tell the truth to.

It dawned on Teddy that this was probably the worst combination in the whole wide world—him and Fowler, that was—but Slocum had put him here, Slocum knew best, and he didn't guess he wanted to fight fate.

18

Out on the Double A spread, the men were still packed at the rail, watching Slocum. In several hours, he'd taken the mare from a bucking, screeching wildcat to what looked like a horse that had been in training forever. She backed when told, came up to have her neck patted, and wore a saddle.

He hadn't been on her yet, but he figured he might get up there today—pretty damn fast for a range horse, if he did say so himself. He knew there were those among the onlookers who disagreed with him. They had made themselves known through the day with catcalls or whispers that sent a shiver of suppressed laughter through the throng.

But Slocum ignored them. He was happy with the mare's progress, and apparently, so was Hawk. He'd spent most of the day leaning against the fence, hat in his hands, grinning in approval.

It was time. Slocum had already saddled the mare, and lunged her in it. She didn't buck anymore. She was becoming resigned to it, as she had become resigned to the halter, and then the bridle that Slocum had introduced a few hours back. She was a fast learner. Just being worked from the ground, she'd already learned to move off, stop, and back up on voice commands. Now he hoped that she didn't buck like a bull once he was in the saddle.

He brought her to the center of the paddock again and sacked her out for the third time since noon. She didn't flinch, didn't move a muscle, though he flapped the blanket every possible place around and on her. Good. He picked up her hooves and held them, one by one, as a farrier would do one day, and looked in her mouth. She was only three, he concluded from the teeth.

And then he returned to her left side and pulled himself up, laying across her, halfway into the saddle.

She shifted beneath him, but that was all. He tried it again. Same result. "Well, young lady, they say that the third time's the charm. What you think, huh?"

He gave her neck a pat, then slowly swung up into the saddle, all the time talking to her. When he was in the saddle with feet firmly in the stirrups and his reins slack, he said softly, "Git up, girl."

She didn't move. "Go on, girl, git up," he repeated, and applied pressure with his knees.

And then she was off. She crow-hopped once, thought it over, and that was the end of it. She never bucked again, so far as Slocum knew. He rode her around the paddock at a walk, then a trot, then a canter, then a walk again, all on a loose rein. When he dismounted, a cheer rose up from the boys and he had to grin. He stroked the mare's neck again, then pulled off her saddle. Once it was off, she shook herself like a wet dog and whinnied. Slocum's already present grin turned into a laugh. Then he stripped her of the bridle, put her halter back on, and led her to the gate.

Where he met up with all the hands who'd been watching. "Good goin', Quincy!" "I never seed the like!" "Some show!" The congratulations came in rapid fire, and he had no idea who said what to him, but at least he remembered he was supposed to be Quincy.

Someone opened the gate, and he led the mare back to the other pen with several of the men still crowded around. The mare made no attempt to bite or kick anybody, and when the gate was opened for her, she went back in with the other broncs off the range.

He closed the gate behind her, rigged the latch, and turned around to find himself facing the last stragglers. "I ain't never seen nothin like that, not ever, Quincy!" said Shorty, who had materialized sometime during the day.

"Why, thanks, Shorty," Slocum said.

Hawk was next. "Tellin' you true, Quincy, I was preparin' to laugh my ass off, but you surely did prove me wrong! What do you call what you did today?"

"You serious?"

"Yeah, I'm serious!"

Slocum took off his hat and gave it a good whack against his leg to knock the dust off. "Just called gentlin', Hawk. Jus' gentlin'."

They began to walk toward the bunkhouse.

Hawk said, "Well, it's still quite a trick."

Hawk's tone was congratulatory, but on this subject, Slocum was like a dog with a bone. "Oh, no trick to it. No trick at all. Any man jack on the place with half a grain'a horse sense could do the same. Do it tomorrow."

Hawk stopped in his tracks. "You joshin' me?"

Slocum shook his head.

They came to the bunkhouse door, where Slocum could smell something good cooking. And see the knot of gabbing hands inside.

Hawk whistled for attention, and pretty soon the men were quiet. "Quincy, here, tells me that any man could do what he did today. I got any takers?"

"Hell, I'll try anythin'," said a medium-sized, towheaded man in a red plaid shirt. "That was sure somethin', Quincy."

"All right," Hawk said, "there's one. Who's next?"

In the end, he had five volunteers, and Slocum was delighted to have that many. He figured that, if they worked hard, they could have those horses rough-broke by the end of the week, and clean-broke by the next weekend. He was content.

On that level anyway. But he still hadn't forgotten his primary reason for being out here.

Somebody hollered, "Supper's ready!" and that made Slocum forget damn near everything else. He'd been working all day and he hadn't eaten since breakfast, and he was hungry enough to eat a skinned skunk.

He took a seat at the table and within seconds had a big plate of beef stew in front of him, with sourdough biscuits and butter and jam on the side.

"This is more like it," he muttered, and focused all his attention on the stew.

By nightfall, Teddy had finished up at the store and was making his way to the café, where he intended to take his supper. While he entered the restaurant, was seen to a table, and ordered, he thought over his day. It hadn't been bad, not bad at all. And he'd done well. Mr. Fowler had said so several times.

Teddy had done well, and he was proud of himself. And he had remembered, off and on throughout the day. He remembered going to school, to Miss Birdsong. He remembered Mr. Fuels at the dairy, and how he used to pay a nickel to any boy who brought in one of his stray cows.

He recalled his first date and his first kiss, and the first time he'd ever made love. That was to Julia Madden, who lived down the road from his family. He recalled that she was awful pretty, and that he'd had a crush on her for the longest time. And that not two weeks after they made love beneath the California moon, she up and married Mingo Cortez, whose family owned the most land in the whole of their county.

He didn't remember much after that, just unconnected snatches here and there, but it was the most he'd recalled in quite some time.

He'd have to tell Slocum, he thought, grinning.

Now wouldn't he get a hoot out of that!

Evening settled over the Double A, and the hands played cards at the dinner table, or talked among themselves at the cots. Slocum sat surrounded by the five men who'd volunteered to try gentling their horses on the morrow. There were plenty of questions, all of which Slocum answered as best he could.

"You gotta get 'em snubbed first," he said, "and then you just do what I done. Keep talkin' to 'em, all soft and croony-like."

"Why?" asked several of the men at once.

"Settles 'em," Slocum said. "Don't ask me why, it just does."

"And then we do the halter first?" Shorty asked.

Slocum nodded. "Once you figure they've bucked themselves out fightin' the post. But keep talkin'. Always keep talkin'. Keep your voice low and even. And when that's settled in, you can unrope 'em from the post."

The questions kept coming and coming, and Slocum kept answering as best he could until he held both arms up. "Now, listen here, fellas. Each horse is different, just like people are. They each got their own special things to be scared of or things to like, and you gotta get inside the horse's head to figure him out. See?"

Shorty seemed to, but the others looked puzzled.

Slocum sighed. "Now, I ain't done with that little bay mare yet. She's gonna take some finishin', some time under saddle outside the pen. And even then, she's gonna need polishin'. But so far as the main things are concerned, after tomorrow, any of you could throw a leg over her and go round up strays."

He lit another ready-made. "Gentlin' is the best way, 'cause it don't break a horse's spirit. Spirit is somethin' you *want* in a horse, same's you want in a woman. If you're a real man, that is."

The sea of heads bobbed as one. Good.

"Now some fellers'll tell you to whip a horse till all the mean's gone out of it. Balderdash! A horse ain't naturally mean, it's man what makes it that way. That's cruelty comin' back to bite you in the butt." He took another puff and saw, to his dismay, that the ready-made was almost half burnt up.

"Aw, Christ on a crutch!" he muttered before he heard Hawk's voice. It surprised him, since Hawk had left the bunkhouse quite a while back. Slocum had figured him to have a separate sleeping place, being the foreman and all.

Hawk stepped forward, grinning. "How late you fellers gonna keep poor Quincy up talkin'? The man's tired, boys. Ease off for tonight, okay?"

Grumbling, the group broke up and the members headed for their own cots. Slocum noticed that Shorty and a hand named Weaver sat on their cots, still hashing over the day's events.

Hawk let out a sigh, then sat down on the end of Slocum's cot. "You made a mighty big mark on them boys today," he said. "Hell, you made a mighty big mark on me!"

Slocum, grinning, lit his last ready-made of the night.

"Don't mind tellin' you that it put a pretty big dent in Heber, too."

Slocum cocked a brow. "How so?"

"I mean, he was real impressed. Reckon he'll wander down sometime tomorrow and have a look-see." Slocum couldn't quite read his expression, but he thought it was close to disdain.

Slocum smiled. "Always glad to have the boss get a look-see." He'd like to get a look-see at the boss, too.

Hawk stood up. "Well, I'll see you in the morning, Quincy. Mighty glad to have you workin' here." And he was out the door, just like that.

Slocum stubbed out his smoke, lay all the way down, and pulled his hat down low, over his eyes. Hawk had given him a good excuse to sack in early, and he was going to take it. He hated to admit it, but that little bay mare had taken the starch right out of him.

He closed his eyes, and despite all the men moving about and talking and laughing, he went to sleep almost at once.

Stretched out on his cot, the covers drawn up tight and his head cradled on his thin pillow, Teddy dreamt. He dreamt of Sally, and a hardware store, and Sally bringing him his lunch, and the hardware store with his name on it, and then "& SON." and then "& SONS." And going home to Sally each night, Sally with her ample charms, Sally with her golden smile, Sally who cooked like a bat outta hell.

He was happy. And in his sleep, he smiled.

19

The next day, at around three in the afternoon, Heber showed up down at the breaking pens.

Slocum didn't see him at first. He had his mare saddled and tied to the fence, having just completed a three-hour ride on the range and put some more manners on her. The other five boys were working their horses in circles, either inside or outside the pen. Everything was going smoothly, or so it seemed.

Slocum leaned back against a corral post and lit a ready-made. He took a draw on it, and that was when he saw Heber, talking to Hawk. Heber didn't look any too pleased.

Oh well, Slocum thought. *Another day, another damn fight to break up.*

He threw down his cigarette prematurely, and started walking toward Heber and Hawk.

"Afternoon, fellers!" he called, his voice sounding chipper.

They turned toward him. Hawk looked relieved. Heber

looked . . . Slocum couldn't tell for certain, but it wasn't too good.

Just as Slocum reached them, Heber said, "I understand you're responsible for this?" He made "this" sound like Slocum had spread horse shit all over his parlor carpet, then asked to be paid for his labor.

But Slocum acted like nothing was wrong, like he didn't want to put his fist right through Heber's narrow, smug face just on general principle, and said, "Yessir, I reckon so. Boys're doin' a good job, ain't they?"

Heber didn't answer. Instead, he looked at Hawk and said, "I want this foolishness stopped immediately. Do you understand?"

"Yessir, but—"

"Right now!" Heber fairly shouted. "We'll break the new horses the same way we always have. None'a this 'gentling' foolishness."

Slocum stepped forward and stared down into Heber's face. "My name's Quincy," he said with assurance, "and if you'll let us keep on, with all the other men assigned, we can finish that whole corral off by Saturday." He signaled to one of the men to bring up his bay mare. "Started working with this filly yesterday. Wild as a kite. You can see how she is now."

He took the mare's reins and pulled her closer, let her get a whiff of Heber as well as Hawk. She obviously liked Hawk a whole lot better than Heber, who said, "Hawk, climb up. I want to see her in action." He looked more like he wanted to see Hawk bucked off and break a leg.

Hawk shot a look at Slocum, but put his boot in the stirrup anyway, and swung up. The mare didn't move a foot, but craned her head around to make certain it wasn't Slocum who'd just mounted her. Slocum stroked her neck and said, "Good girl, good girl, somebody new to ride you for a while, all right?"

To Hawk, he just said, "I'm startin' her on the neck rein. She's doin' pretty good, but she still slips up every once in a while. Ride patient. Easy on the bit."

Hawk, bless him, knew just what to do. He hadn't been studying Slocum's every move all day yesterday and today for nothing.

He trotted the mare out to an open place, and began to ride her in large circles. Then he began to figure-eight her at a lope, making flying lead changes. He stopped her, then backed her up about twenty feet, then spun her in a reining circle a few times. All the other men had stopped to watch, and when he finished, they all cheered. Hawk doffed his hat and bowed in the saddle.

He rode back to Slocum and Heber, then dismounted, saying, "By God, Quincy!" He stroked the mare's neck. "I ain't been on a horse this nice since I was a kid, back home in Virginny!"

Heber turned toward Slocum. "How do I know this horse ain't a ringer?"

Ain't a ringer? thought Slocum. *Seems when Heber thinks he's lost an argument, he loses control of proper English diction, too.*

Slocum opened his mouth, but Hawk beat him to it.

"You was right there when we brung these broncs in off the range, Heber. You said yourself that you didn't never see a rougher sting."

Heber stared a hole in the ground before he said, "Oh, all right! By Saturday, then!" He turned on his heel and stomped off toward the house.

Slocum blew out air between pursed lips. "Now, there's a man you don't mind seein' the back of!"

Hawk laughed with such vigor that he spooked the bay, and Slocum quickly stepped in to quiet her. "You're a man who knows his horses," Slocum said.

"Naw, nothin' like you," Hawk answered. "What I said to Heber was the God's honest truth." He stroked the mare's neck again. "I think maybe we'll call you Wren. Any objections, Quincy?"

Slocum smiled. "Wren. I think I like it."

"Wren it is, then!"

Meanwhile, Teddy had been busy gathering information between selling shovels, paint, and fencing. From Mrs. Halliday, he'd learned that everyone in town—except maybe the Hendricks family—had been very upset about Mr. McAlister's passing, but weren't so crazy about Heber taking over.

"He married Dora, you know. She was Mr. McAlister's only child." She dabbed at her eyes, adding, "Dora passed away not two days after her daddy. Doc said it was grief, just plain grief what did her in."

Teddy had expressed sympathy, then asked, "If you folks all liked Dora and her daddy so much, what is there about this Heber you don't like?"

"I'll never in my life understand why Dora married him in the first place. He's nasty and highfalutin, that's it. Just plain nasty and highfalutin! What do we owe for the reels of wire?"

Slocum had told him the best place to find gossip from women was the hairdresser's or the seamstress's shop. Wait till Slocum heard what you could learn clerking in a hardware store!

He'd also gathered, from Ernie Biggs and Mr. Wheeler, that they didn't care for Heber either, and couldn't figure why Mr. McAlister had hired him the first place. Unless Heber had something on him, that was. Both men suggested that, Ernie Biggs especially.

Ernie had almost broken a jar filled with No. 4 nails that sat on the counter, he was so vehement.

Teddy thought he'd done a good job of being discreet, and when anybody asked why he wanted to know, he just told them that his brother, John, had signed on to the ranch roster to break horses for them.

That seemed to satisfy those who questioned.

Mrs. Halliday had said, "Well, if I was your brother, I'd up and quit as soon as possible. That Heber's a devil!"

After each person who'd given him a clue—well, maybe they weren't clues exactly, he wasn't sure—left the shop, he pulled out a little pad of paper and a pencil stub that Slocum had left for him, and wrote down the information, and the person's name.

He was a good little sniffin' hound, Slocum would have said.

Before nightfall, all the men who'd been gentling horses were up on them, riding in gentle circles and cooing nonstop to their mounts. Slocum had worked Wren a bit more. He hadn't gotten around to teaching the ground tie yet, but he figured he'd put that on her tomorrow. She'd worked enough for one day, and was as tired as he was.

He put Wren into a stall—a first for her, he imagined—then grained and watered her and threw a flake of hay into her manger.

"Don't fight it, girl, or there'll be hell to pay for both of us," he said, giving her a last stroke.

He walked back up to where the men were working horses. He was proud of every single one of them. They'd followed instructions to the dot. And he could tell they were proud of themselves, too. Oh, there was going to be plenty of bragging in the bunkhouse tonight!

And as for the hangers-back—the men who hadn't volunteered—they were down there, too, every man jack of them. And the consensus of opinion was that if their buddies could do it without so much as getting kicked or bitten once, so could they.

Slocum found this pretty entertaining. These were men who would willingly climb on a bronc with no schooling, no gentling, and try to stay in the saddle while that bronc bucked, turned, and hopped like nobody's business. But they'd been afraid of a little ground work first.

Well, he thought, *change comes hard sometimes.*

He found himself standing beside Hawk. He said, "You got a good crew, Hawk. I'd be plenty proud of 'em if I was you."

Hawk nodded. "I am. Did I tell you that every single one'a them come up and asked me could they give this deal a try tomorrow?"

"You didn't, but I'm right glad to hear it. And if'n you want'a know, if we get all these boys to put as much heart into it as the first five, we'll have all those broncs ladybroke by Friday."

Hawk's brows shot up. "No kiddin'?"

"That's the way I see 'er."

Laughter bubbled up Hawk's throat. "That'll sure piss off ol' Heber! He's all 'conquer or destroy,' don't believe in this gentling nonsense. Well, you met 'im. You ever run into a nastier piece of business?"

"Can't say as I have," Slocum lied. "How'd he get along with the old boss? Mr. McAlister, right?"

"Yeah, McAlister. That was sure a shame, him gettin' killed like that."

Slocum asked him how it happened, and Hawk spent the next hour telling him. Sort of.

"You seem a little creaky on the details," Slocum said when they were on their way to the bunkhouse. "You keep tellin' me what Heber said. Weren't there nobody else there to see it?"

Hawk opened the bunkhouse door, and Slocum followed him in. By the scent of it, it was beef stew again.

Hawk said, "I'll tell you the truth, Quincy. I don't believe a word'a what I just told you. Not really. Now, there was bad blood between McAlister and the whole of the Hendricks clan. They bought a piece of land up in the hills a ways, and found out they controlled the water rights. Didn't make no difference, so far as the Hendrickses was concerned. What were they gonna do, dam the whole river? But McAlister had a bug up his butt about it. Finally got the property out from under 'em. But old man Hendricks never forgave him, and Mr. McAlister swore he'd shoot any Hendricks he found on his land." Hawk paused while they sat down at the table.

"Guess maybe that Hendricks that crossed his land figured to fire first," Hawk continued. "I dunno. I lived here most'a my born days, and I never had no problems with the Hendrickses. I got to be good friends with their son, Jonas. I just can't believe that he done it. Jonas wouldn't hurt a rattler, lest it was in the process of strikin' him." He shook his head. "There was a deputy killed, too. You hear about that?"

Slocum shook his head.

"Well, he was leadin' the posse that went after Jonas Hendricks. Dale Henderson. Good man. They opened fire on Jonas, and Deputy Dale took a slug to the head. Died straight off. But I got a question for you, Quincy. How does a feller with only a handgun, shootin' from three hundred yards away, leave powder burns behind?"

Slocum wrinkled his brow. "Impossible," he said. "He'd have to be shot from up close for powder burns. And hell, a handgun wouldn't be worth shit from three hundred yards!"

Hawk just solemnly nodded. "What I said. To myself anyhow, lest I be the next. And then there's Dora."

"Dora?"

"McAlister's daughter. She kicked two days after the thing with Hendricks. Heber said she died from grievin' over her pa, but I don't think so. Not Dora. She was a strong woman, real strong in both mind 'n body. Right handsome, too."

Softly Slocum asked, "What are you sayin' exactly?"

Nothing. And then, from Slocum's other side, came Shorty's hushed voice. "It was Heber, Quincy. That's what we're all thinkin'. Heber done all three of 'em in, sure as shootin'."

"Shut up, Shorty!" Hawk hissed.

"It was Heber," Shorty said again, and dove into his stew.

"Sometimes I get to wonderin' why I brung you out here in the first place, Shorty," Hawk said.

"To keep that skinny ass'a yours honest," came Shorty's curt reply. Then he smiled. "Good stew."

20

The following day, and the day after that, and the day after *that*, they broke horses. Things were splendid, so far as Slocum was concerned. The men, most of them, were good hands with horses and fell right into the rhythm of the thing without hardly any coaching at all. Most of the horses were finished, and they all had been trained to ground tie and have their hooves handled, which Slocum figured the blacksmith would appreciate. Best of all, he'd saved a few more horses from the hard-handed practice known as "bronc busting," and hopefully at least some of these boys would pass it on.

Hawk was beside himself with glee. "You know what, Quincy? I figure you saved us almost a month's work, sharin' that gentlin' business. I always got that to throw in Heber's face if'n he gets all uppity with me."

Slocum smiled and hooked an elbow over the top rail of the fence. "That you can. I believe I done myself outta a job, though. I only signed on for breakin' horses, and looks

to me like your boys can take care of it from here on out."
But he was thinking, *More like you told me what I needed to know, and now I'm gonna report in to Pete down in Phoenix.*

"What? Anybody who can handle horses like that can surely teach us somethin' about cows!"

Slocum shook his head, and hugged the rail that much tighter. "Nope. I'm not a cattleman. Jus' lemme know where a plate of it's at, and I'm on it like a bluebottle fly on a bucket'a gizzards. But that's it. Sorry." But secretly, he had enjoyed schooling these boys in the way of gentling horses, enjoyed their admiration, and enjoyed seeing them come to respect themselves in the process. There probably *was* a lot he could teach them about managing cattle, too. But the plain truth of it was that his real business here was done, and it was time to ride south again.

He figured Teddy would be pleased, at least. He hoped the kid had dug up something in town, too. And he hoped that Jonas Hendricks wasn't pacing a groove in the floor of that cell, down in Phoenix.

And then he figured that maybe he could phone the marshal's office from here. He hadn't seen a telephone in the marshal's office, but they had a railroad station that he hadn't set foot in. There, he would very likely find a telephone. He hoped. The sweetest thing would be if Pete told him to pick up Heber right then, and bring him on down. Kill two birds with one stone, so to speak.

"I gotta get movin'," said Slocum, who had only paused to talk to Hawk on his way down to the barn to rescue Ace from his life of leisure. He'd been locked up down there for almost five days, and Slocum figured he'd have a whole lot of hoppy toad to get out of his system.

Hawk shook his head sadly. "If you gotta . . . But if you're around this time next year, stop by. There'll be a new string to break, and half the hands will've been run off by Heber's rotten nature—"

Slocum nodded. "I'll keep it in mind, Hawk. Thanks."

Hawk suddenly threw both hands in the air. "Hell, I forgot I gotta pay you, Quincy! You go get that wild-colored horse'a yours, and I'll go get your money."

"Sounds like a plan," Slocum said, and set off for the horse barn.

When he rode into town again, the first thing he did was to stop by the hardware and check on Teddy.

And he was astonished when the boy seemed none too eager to quit his job!

"I got all kinds'a dirt, Slocum," Teddy whispered. "Got it writ down on paper, too." He produced the little notepad, now dark with his scrawl. Six pages were full of it.

"Can I borrow this?" Slocum asked him.

"Sure," Teddy answered, but there was a question in his eyes.

"Gonna go to the depot and try to find a telephone," Slocum said by way of explanation.

Teddy nodded, and Slocum went on up the street, which was just as empty as the day they rode into town. The depot wasn't showing any signs of activity either. There wasn't a horse hitched to the rail or a buggy waiting, so it must not be any time close to a stop.

He climbed down and tied Ace to the rail, even though the place looked deader than a doornail. He walked up to the door and gave it a little tap with his knuckles. Just enough to rattle the glass. When nobody answered, he tried the knob. It opened right up.

"Anybody home?" he shouted.

"Geez, mister!" The sound had come from below the counter's height, and the boy that stood up behind it—no

older than seventeen or eighteen, with sandy hair and a
scraggly mustache—looked plain scared.

"Calm down, kid," Slocum said. "Just wanted t'know if
you had a telephone I could use."

The boy calmed visibly, and said, "Yeah, over here. It's
a dime a minute, though."

Slocum smiled. "Who keeps the clock on me?"

The boy cleared his throat nervously. "I—I—I do, mister. I start timin' you from the time you start talkin'."

Slocum nodded. "Sounds fair. You the telegrapher, too?"

The boy nodded.

"You got a name?"

"Yessir. John Quincy Carpenter."

Slocum nearly buckled over, laughing. "Small world,"
he finally managed. He walked right up to the counter and
stuck out his hand. "I'm John Quincy." And then, remembering that he'd need to identify himself to Pete, said,
"Slocum. John Quincy Slocum."

The kid lit up. "I'll be danged! Another John Quincy!
Now, if that don't beat everythin'!"

Slocum smiled. "The phone?"

"Oh, yeah. Hang on just a second . . ."

That evening, Slocum and Teddy sat in the café, discussing
events and plans over beef and noodles, served with honey
and biscuits and coleslaw.

Slocum had made his call and got hold of Pete, reporting
what he knew, plus the things in Teddy's notes. He was
surprised that Teddy had managed to glean so much information, and told him so.

"T'weren't nothin'," Teddy said, shrugging. "And you
was wrong to tell me the best places for lady gossip's the
hairdresser's and the dressmaker's. It's the goddamn hardware store! Ladies'll tell a nice young feller, sellin' them

paint and such, most anythin'. Never seen the like, Sl—I mean, John." Embarrassed, he forked a wad of coleslaw into his mouth. The dressing dribbled down his chin.

"Well," said Slocum, ignoring Teddy's mess, "told Pete everything—least, what I could with the telegraph clerk hangin' on my every word—and he says for us to go collect ol' Heber and bring him down to Phoenix. In chains, if necessary. He's sending up a few deputy marshals to do some more investigatin' once we get Heber outta the way."

"Neat!" Teddy said.

Slocum had taken the time to start chewing another mouthful of noodles and beef before Teddy's curt reply. He'd counted on it being longer. He finished chewing, and swallowed.

"Teddy, you make it sound like it's gonna be all fun an' games. This Heber, he's killed three people inside the last few weeks, includin' his wife! I don't think he's gonna get all sentimental over takin' a few potshots at us."

"Well, don't we have to be, like, official? To go arrest him, I mean."

"Yes, we do. I got deputized before we left Phoenix. Got a badge for you in my pocket. I'll deputize you tonight, after we get back to the hotel."

"Me? A deputy marshal?" Teddy's brows shot up in astonishment. "For true?"

"Shh." Slocum waved him down, both in volume and in height, because he was halfway standing inside a second. "Keep your voice down and your ass in that chair," Slocum hissed. "Don't go givin' us away now!"

There was not much chance of that. The café was, for the tiny town, crowded this night, and the air was full of the buzz of conversation.

"Like I said, we'll get you deputized tonight, and come morning, we'll take a ride out to the Double A and pick up

Heber. He's prob'ly gonna go kickin' and screamin', but he'll go. Just watch yourself, okay?"

Teddy thought about it for a minute. "Okay. I got you." For a few moments, they were both quiet as they ate their suppers. And then Teddy surprised the hell out of Slocum by asking, right out of the clear blue sky, "You ever think about gettin' hitched?"

Slocum was lost for words. He just shook his head.

"You think it's right for a feller to marry a whore?" he asked solemnly. "I mean, if he loves her and everything, and she loves him back, and he can make a livin' to support her?"

Slocum studied him. "Why you askin'?"

"I been missin' Sally, missin' her somethin' terrible. I think if I asked her, she'd say yes. And when we divvy up the reward money, it'll be enough that I can go into business with my half. I already done a lot'a dreamin' about it."

Slocum truly didn't know what to say. Teddy had actually thought about this, thought it through, so far as Slocum could see. Except . . . "What kind'a store you figure to open?"

"Hardware," came the answer. "But you didn't answer my question. About Sally. About me marryin' her."

Quite suddenly, Slocum heard himself say, "Fine by me. I wish you the best'a luck, kid. Mean that."

All the nervousness went out of Teddy, and his grin was practically ear-to-ear. "I love her, Slocum, I mean, I really love her, and I hope she loves me even half as much."

"Well, you're sure enthusiastic, I'll say that for you," Slocum said, then ordered himself another cup of coffee. At least Sally was one of the few girls at Katie's who hadn't come on to Slocum. He figured that gave her a few extra points. And she was a pretty little redhead, with a sexy little pout, a pert nose, and blue, blue eyes fringed with dark lashes.

She and Teddy would make some pretty babies, all right.

21

"I do," Teddy said, one hand on the Bible and the other raised, palm out.

Slocum nodded. "Congratulations, Deputy," he said, and pinned the badge onto Teddy's proud chest. The kid was trembling with excitement.

To tell the truth, Slocum was getting quite a kick out of the proceedings. He'd been temporarily sworn in a heap of times, but he was never the one doing the swearing in of somebody else. He was tickled to be doing it, but he still took the whole process very seriously. It meant a lot, that deputy marshal's badge, no matter which side of it you were on. And Slocum knew. He'd been on both sides of it.

When he had finished the pinning, Teddy grinned wide and said, "Hot damn! Thanks, Slocum! I don't think . . . I don't think I ever been this proud!"

Slocum couldn't help smiling at him and nodding. "It's a big responsibility, that badge. You remember that, okay?"

"I will," said Teddy. He paused a moment. "Slocum?

From now on, I'd appreciate it if you'd start callin' me Ted."

Slocum nodded. "All right, Ted. Be happy to do it for you."

"Good, then." Teddy fingered his badge, then looked up. "Be much obliged."

Long after Teddy had gone to his room for the night, Slocum sat by the window, smoking. He'd had the presence of mind to buy a fresh pack down at the general store when he'd picked up Teddy. He smiled to himself. *No, that's Ted to you, Slocum.*

Anyway, the cigarettes weren't the right brand and they tasted just slightly of cow piss, but they were still better than rolling his own. Maybe he was just losing his taste for quirlies.

He looked down at the street. The town was pretty much boarded up for the night. But he'd bet that Ted was still up, and still staring at the badge.

It was funny. Here, Teddy had been a wanted man, robbed stages and killed people, and not much more than a month later, he'd pinned on the same badge the man he'd killed had worn, and he wore it reverently. Again, Slocum found himself hoping like hell that Teddy wouldn't remember, not ever. And that if he did, he'd suck it up like a man and keep the information to himself.

Be better for everybody.

Except maybe that Alice Swan. Why the hell'd she have to pop out of the woodwork again anyhow? And what kind of a line of work was this for a woman? It didn't make any sense to him.

They'd pick up Heber in the morning. Easier said than done, and certainly a whole lot tougher than Teddy—no, that was Ted—was imagining it to be.

But then, Teddy brought Slocum luck. Because of Teddy, Slocum had shot Wash Trumble. Because of Teddy, he'd gotten to visit Miss Katie more times in a month than he usually did in a couple of years. Because of Ted, he had a whole pocket full of notes and names and places.

Maybe Ted was right. Maybe it'd be easy.

He genuinely hoped so.

The next morning, they set off for the Double A. Once again, Slocum noted the peacefulness of the ride. It was along the edge of the woods, and birdsong filled the clear, clean air. He had a feeling this was the last bit of peace he was going to experience today.

Before they left town, he had told Ted to take off his badge and put it in his pocket for the time being—he could always produce it later—for there was no sense in alerting Heber to what was coming. Slocum had already slipped his into his vest pocket.

He hoped he was right. He hoped they could ride right up to the house, knock on the door, arrest Heber, and that would be that.

But he knew things didn't generally work out like you wanted, or even like you hoped.

They took the final curve south, and soon had ridden to the clearing—actually, an island of dust in a sea of grass— where the ranch was located. The hacienda itself really impressed Ted. He sat his mare with his jaw hanging open, and all that came out was, "Gosh!"

Slocum replied, "Yeah, ain't it somethin'?"

"Not worth takin' three lives," Ted replied. This was the same boy who'd taken three lives himself, and for just their watches and pocket change, Slocum noted, though he said nothing.

"Well, what now?" Ted asked. He was getting antsy,

shifting back and forth in the saddle and fiddling with his reins.

"We go in," Slocum replied, calm as a windless pond and sober as a judge.

They rode straight up to the house, tied their horses to the rail, and went to the front door. Slocum had just lifted his knuckles to knock when a shout came from behind him.

"Hey, Quincy! You should come see how good that sorrel gelding'a mine's doin'!" It was Shorty.

"Maybe later?" Slocum called.

Shorty nodded. "Good t'be seein' you! I'll tell Hawk you're here!"

"Shorty, don't—" Slocum started, but Shorty was already down by the corral, and didn't hear him. "Shit," he muttered.

Just about the time he turned back toward the door, it opened, and there stood Heber, eyeing him curiously with those narrow-set eyes of his. To call him hatchet-faced would have been a compliment.

Instead of *What can I help you with?* or *What can I do for you?* or even *Good Morning*, he just sneered, "What?" Distaste fairly oozed from him.

Slocum subtly moved his foot into the door. "Heber Johnson?" he asked.

"Who else?" came the mean-spirited reply.

Slocum scowled. He could be just as nasty as this boy. He said, "My name's Slocum, and I'm with the U.S. marshal's office. I'm here to arrest you for the murders of Mr. Ebenezer McAlister, Deputy Dale Henderson, and Mrs. Dora Johnson, and the attempted railroading of one Jonas Hendricks."

Heber's expression changed to one of shock, and the first thing he did was to try to slam the door.

That plan didn't get very far, because the door met with both Slocum's foot and the weight of Ted's shoulder, then Slocum's weight as they pushed the door open instead of closed.

Heber took off down the tile-floored front hall, his thin knees knocking, but Slocum drew and fired a shot. He stopped immediately to stare at the place where the figurine Slocum had just shot had stood. All that remained on the table were a few chips of porcelain.

"Philistine! Idiot!" Heber shouted. "That was Ming Dynasty!"

Ted, standing with arms folded, said, "Now it's Blown-Up Dynasty. Got anythin' else you want exploded or shot?"

Slowly, Heber shook his head, and Slocum handed the cuffs, also on loan from Pete, to Teddy. No, it really was Ted now, he realized. The kid had changed, gone from a bloodthirsty boy to a grown-up man, ready to marry and settle down, in a little more than a month's time. It was pretty damn amazing, when you thought about it.

Ted moved forward and cuffed Heber behind the back, then said, "C'mon, killer," and walked him back to Slocum just as somebody else pounded on the door.

Slocum opened it. Hawk stood outside, hat in his hands. Slocum said, "Howdy, Hawk."

Surprised to have Slocum open the door, Hawk said, "Hey, Quincy. Say, if you were goin' to bring back that extra I slipped into your envelope, you should'a come down to . . ." He trailed off as, looking past Slocum's bulk, he saw his boss in handcuffs. "What you doin', Quincy?" he demanded.

"Calm down, Hawk," he replied, and slipped his badge from his pocket. He pinned it to his shirt. "First off, my name's not Quincy. It's Slocum, and I'm with the U.S. marshal's office. Meet my partner, Ted."

Ted, keeping a firm hand on Heber's elbow, nodded seriously.

Slocum continued, "We came out this mornin' to arrest your boss, here, for murder. Three murders, actually, and one attempted. There's gonna be a couple more deputy marshals comin' up from Phoenix to search the house and question all the hands, I reckon. Don't worry. Me and Ted, we don't suspect anybody else of any wrongdoin'."

Hawk was flabbergasted, and just stood there, with his hat in his hands, stuttering, "B-but what ab-bout the ranch?" he finally got out.

Slocum put a hand on his shoulder. "Just keep it runnin' like usual. Be a while before the court figures out what to do with it, I reckon."

Hawk, reduced to silence, just nodded.

"Mind gettin' his horse tacked up, so's he don't have to walk back to town? We're takin' him down on the eleven-fifteen, so somebody can pick it up after that."

Hawk regained his composure. "Where?"

"At the livery. That okay with you?"

"Ain't nothin' about this that seems right. But I guess." He turned around and hollered, "Hey, Shorty! Get Heber's saddle horse tacked up and bring him up here, would you?"

Shorty, who was halfway down to the horse barn, hollered back, "Why?"

Hawk shouted impatiently, "Tell you later. Now hurry your ass up!"

Shorty took off at a trot.

Five minutes later, he was leading a flashy palomino gelding up to the porch. And when Slocum and Ted brought Heber down the steps and helped him up on his horse, Shorty nearly fell right down.

"H-Hawk?" he asked.

"Tell you later. Slocum, you'd best be takin' those reins. Old Goldie, here, he's trained to knee rein."

It was the closest Hawk had come to helping with the capture, and it was merely a subtle warning, but Slocum nodded and said, "Thanks, Hawk. 'Preciate it."

"You'll pay for this," Heber hissed from atop the palomino. "You'll all pay!"

Ted handed the reins to Slocum as he said, "Oh, shut up," to Heber. He mounted his horse. "Let's go, Slocum. We're burnin' daylight."

Slocum smiled at him. Yeah, he was pretty damn amazing, all right. Slocum threw a leg over Ace, and the three of them headed back toward town.

22

The train ride down to Phoenix was uneventful, although Ted turned back into Teddy for the minutes it took him to buy licorice from the porter and wolf it down.

Heber sat quietly. Slocum couldn't tell whether he had seen the futility in it and had just given up, or whether he was sitting there, quietly plotting. Slocum kept his Colt in hand, though, just in case.

Pete and two other fellows met them at the station when they got down to Phoenix. Turned out the fellows were deputy marshals, and they took Heber into custody right then and there. Slocum took off his badge and handed it to Pete. "Reckon you'll want this back," he said. "Thanks for the loan of it."

"Slocum, don't. I'd like to hire you. I mean, on account of you, we got the real killer! Be proud to put you on the payroll."

But Slocum pressed the badge on him anyway. "Sorry, Pete. I can make a whole lot more money bounty huntin' than I could fillin' out forms in the office. 'Sides, you don't pay nothin' to your boys when they pick up a fugitive."

"Why, sure we do!" Pete argued. "We might not pay the full bounty, but then again, you get yourself a regular paycheck. All evens out in the end."

"For the last time, no," Slocum said, placing a friendly hand on Pete's shoulder. "I been doin' what I do for a long time, don't try to change me now!"

Pete just shook his head. He muttered, "Lord knows I tried."

"You can have mine, too, Marshal," said Ted as he handed over his badge.

Pete quirked a brow. "Why? You thinkin' 'bout goin' into the bounty huntin' trade, too?"

Slocum shook his head. "Nope. He's thinkin' about marryin' himself a wife and openin' a hardware store," he answered proudly.

"Yessir, I am," Teddy added with a grin.

Pete thumbed back his hat. "I'll be damned. I'll just be damned!" He looked at Slocum a good long stare, and then he looked at the ground. "Slocum," he said, at last looking up. "Can I see you in my office?"

Slocum's brow furrowed. He'd been planning on getting back to Katie's first thing. So had Ted. They'd talked about it on the train ride south. He asked, "When?"

"Right now'd be perfect."

Slocum turned to Ted. "You wanna get these horses settled in over to the stable. Grain 'em good. And tell Katie I'm on my way, just gotta take care'a some business, first. Okay?"

Ted nodded, and began untying the train-weary horses from the rail. Slocum thought that Ace had taken it fine, but Ted's mare seemed the worse for wear.

Slocum heard him talking to the horses as he walked off,

leading them. "That's all right, girl. That was a train, and it didn't hurt you a bit, did it? Saved you a lotta countryside, too. See how nice Ace is handlin' it? That's a good, brave Ace . . ."

"Let's go," said Slocum. "Wanna get this over with soon's possible, okay?"

Ted passed on Slocum's message as soon as he walked through Katie's front door, and he was upstairs with Sally within a minute.

Giggling, she said, "Teddy! Did you get your man?"

"In a manner'a talkin'," he replied, caught up in her laughter. "Were you true t'me while I was gone?"

"Sure thing," she said. "Cross my heart."

"Then will you answer me a question?"

She nodded.

"Sally, would you do me the great honor'a marryin' me?"

She looked shocked. And then she began to cry. "F-For real?"

"Sure, for real! I been thinkin' about it for days, even talked it over with Slocum. Thought I'd take my reward money and buy me a store, stock it for hardware. Would you mind bein' a hardware man's wife?"

"Oh, Teddy!" she said before she threw herself into his arms. "I love you so much!"

"Does that mean you will?"

"Yes, yes!" she cried. "Yes, yes, yes!"

He kissed her so hard and deep that he was almost lost inside her.

"Oh, honey, it sounds real excitin', but I don't know how you stand it!" Katie said as she lounged, nude and exhausted, on the bed. Slocum had got back at around five, now it was eleven o'clock, and they hadn't been downstairs since!

"Fact is, if I'd been you, I would'a turned tail and hustled my bustle home the first time I seen him!" she continued.

Slocum said, "Good thing I'm not you!" and laughed. "Wouldn't know how to ride in a bustle!"

"You kill me, Slocum." She waved a hand over to the chair where he was sitting, smoking. Once he'd got back to Phoenix and finished up with Pete's office, he'd gone and bought that tobacconist clean out of those good ready-mades, plus a couple of good cigars. One for him and one for Ted, who as yet hadn't come up for air either. In the meantime, he was smoking the ready-mades.

"You'd look plain silly in a bustle. Besides which, there ain't a more skilled rider in the Arizona Territory than you." Languidly, she rolled to the side and toyed with one of the fancy little embroidered pillows she kept there.

Slocum thought she'd made a mistake to leave out California, Nevada, Colorado, and New Mexico, but he didn't say anything. He guessed that maybe she hadn't been to any of those places.

Even if she had, he'd forgive her. He'd forgive a multitude of sins for anybody with an ass like that, or those two high, silky orbs of breasts. She had a narrow waist and a long neck and no double chin, no sir, with long attractive legs and arms like a ballerina, and a face that . . . a face that could launch a thousand ships, he decided, like the Greek woman that caused that Trojan War way back in the olden times. Helen, they called her. Helen of Troy.

Proud of himself that he'd remembered, he lit another ready-made, using one of Katie's newfangled cigarette lighters. This one was big and silver, and shaped like a lady's tit, and when you pushed a button on the bottom, the nipple opened up, and there was the fire.

It was kind of a poetic thing, when you thought about it. And Slocum had.

He'd been thinking and thinking and thinking, but he was still not marriage material, period. In fact, he loved Katie too much to marry her, to put her through the struggle he knew he'd have with her and himself. Mostly himself. He just wasn't ready to settle down. He supposed he was a little like a big kid, always wanting to find out what—or who—was in the next pond over, and the urge to go check it out was completely irresistible. And that was just the way it was for now. Well, seeing as how it had always been that way, he reckoned it would stay that way to the end.

Young Ted was a lucky cuss, all right. He could actually do what Slocum could only dream about. Maybe Ted was the better man, after all.

"You told Teddy yet? About what the marshal said?" Katie asked, her pretty head tipped to the side.

"Nope. Ain't seen him," Slocum replied. "Gotta see him to tell him." He lit another ready-made.

"Reckon he'll be pleased?"

Slocum sat forward so suddenly he nearly dropped hot ashes on his leg. "Pleased? You joshin' me? That boy, he's gonna be over the moon!"

"So, aren't you happy for him?"

"What?"

"I said, so why aren't you happy for him?"

Slocum shook his head. "I'm plumb tickled for him, Katie. Who wouldn't be?"

She turned back over and sat up, her breasts swaying temptingly with the movement. "You. Don't know why, but you aren't. You come in here all happy, all right, but there's somethin' underneath like a festerin' boil. What is it that's got you so riled up?"

He couldn't tell her. He couldn't say that it was her or Teddy or anything else, really. "I don't know, dammit."

"Well, don't go snappin' at me!"

He sighed. "Sorry, Kate. Didn't mean to. It's just . . . everythin'. Can't explain it. Sorry, I didn't think it showed."

Katie's tone was suddenly soft and silky again. "Poor baby," she crooned, and waved a hand toward him, beckoning him to her bed once more.

But for once, Slocum was in no mood. He just sat there, smoking and brooding, and finally, Katie said, "I'll go down and get more whiskey, all right, honey?"

Slocum nodded, and that was that.

Katie took her leave quietly, her gauzy robe gathered around her and the whiskey decanter thinly swishing in her hand.

While Katie was downstairs, Slocum stubbed out his ready-made and just as quickly lit another. If he'd get himself calmed down, he thought, he'd kill himself. Everything in moderation, his pa used to tell him. Well, everything except women, he'd add when Slocum's mama was out of earshot.

It was rare that he had troubles and didn't even know what they were. Usually he had his finger right on them. Well, usually, the trouble was some jackass shooting at him from up on a ridge or behind a barn or galloping south in one big hurry.

"Life stinks," he muttered, then lit another cigarette anyway. He wished it was stuffed with hemp instead of tobacco. That's how far he'd sunk, wanting to smoke himself full of hemp or opium.

And why should he feel this way? Was it because Pete

had tried to hire him on—again—or that Pete was going to take over watching Ted, if Ted wanted to stay in Phoenix? Was it that he'd miss the kid that much, or was it that he'd miss Katie that much?

Or was it that he had no idea who to go after next? Times were changing. It was almost a whole new century, and the inventions of man were coming so fast and furious he could hardly keep up with them. Telephones, even in the tiniest towns. Kids, riding those big clumsy bicycles in the streets. City baseball teams, trains going right through mountains, and those big, stand-up gizmos like they had over at the saloon, that would play music for a nickel. The Indian tribes were all civilized, even the wildest of them, and robbing stages was a crime on its way out the door, what with there being fewer and fewer runs scheduled. People took the trains nowadays.

Maybe that was it. Too much was changing, and too fast. Maybe he was just plain too old to adapt to it. Maybe he was . . .

No! he told himself. He wasn't too old for anything.

Maybe he ought to make a plan, a plan for his future. He'd never done that before, and the idea of it intrigued him. Hell, Ted had made one. Why couldn't he?

He decided that he could still bounty-hunt. He was still good on a horse, and wasn't so banged up that he couldn't draw his gun in a quarter second flat. Course that might not seem so fast to some fellers, but he had his name. And his name seemed to scare most fellows into just giving in lately.

So, he decided that he could keep bounty hunting for at least a few years more. And then, if the good Lord was willing and the creek didn't rise, he'd come back to Phoenix and settle down. Even marry Katie, if she was still available.

Yes, that would do.

And suddenly, he felt about thirty pounds lighter. He actually felt . . . good!

Stark naked, he stood up and opened the door.

"Katie!!" he bellowed. "Katie, get that rosy butt of yours up here now!"

23

At a little after noon, Slocum, having been out for a morning stroll around the city, was just finishing his lunch when Ted and Sally made an appearance. They looked sleepy but jubilant, and Slocum guessed that her answer had been a resounding *Yes!*

He was right, because the first thing that Ted said, once they were in side-by-side chairs at the table, was, "Slocum, girls, we got an announcement to make!"

A hush fell over the table, Katie included. She had confided in Slocum last night that she'd be a ringtailed polecat if Teddy didn't propose. When asked why, she said she just had a feeling. Women's intuition and all.

"Me and Sally," Ted continued with an air of, well, triumph, "we're gettin' hitched. This afternoon!"

The girls, Katie included, sent up a cheer, and then they were all on their feet, huggin' Sally, hugging Teddy, and breaking out the champagne. Katie came over to his end of the table and gave Slocum a big hug.

"I told you," she said. "Oh, I'm so happy for 'em!"

"Me, too, Katie," Slocum allowed, smiling. "An' I think they got pretty good prospects for the future, too."

He said no more on the subject until everyone was handed a champagne glass, and Katie made a toast, then Slocum. It was decent champagne, but not as good as the bottle Slocum had brought last night. He hoped it was still safe and sound up in the cupboard.

After everyone had broken up, and it was just Katie and him and Sally and Teddy left in the kitchen, he said, "All right, folks. Settle down," and waved everybody into their seats before he sat down, too. "Got some important news for Ted. You, too, Sally."

Katie tipped her head.

"Want you to listen in, Kate," he added, stopping her before she had a chance to stand.

Ted was leaning forward on his forearms. "What is it, Slocum?"

"I made a walkin' tour of the town this mornin', Ted, and I got good news for you. There's a whole new row of shops goin' in over on Adams—nice brick ones, with the stores downstairs an' livin' quarters upstairs, and with—get this—real plumbin'. Toilets for the downstairs and the upstairs, and upstairs a real shower bath and a tub."

Sally began to fan her neck, she was so shaken up with the surprise. She giggled, "Real inside plumbin'! I read about it, but I never thought I'd live to see it!"

Slocum held up his hand. "There's more."

"More?" Sally and Teddy said as one.

Then Teddy added, "What, Slocum? Tell us!"

"Stopped by the marshal's office, too. We don't get paid nothin' for Jonas Hendricks. Fact, Pete already turned him loose. But for ol' Heber, we got three thousand dollars, on account of the third murder we uncovered. Your half'a both

Heber and Wash comes to about five thousand, two hundred and fifty."

Teddy's mouth was hanging open, and Sally, bug-eyed, gasped and covered her mouth.

Slocum reached into a pocket and pulled out a bank envelope. "There's a weddin' present in there from me, too."

Sally had the presence of mind to take the envelope, open it, and begin counting the money. When she was finished, she couldn't speak.

"What, Baby?" Ted asked. "What is it? Are you all right?"

"Thi-thi-this is t-t-ten thousand dollars, Teddy!" she finally managed before she just threw her arms around him and wept.

Beside Slocum, Katie whispered, "Ten thousand?"

Slocum shrugged. "Thought I'd make it an even number," he said.

Katie laughed and shook her head. "You kill me, Slocum, I mean, sometimes you just honest-to-God kill me!"

Slocum stayed on a few more days, figuring out where to go next, and helping Teddy get his shop picked out and paid for. It was a nice one, right on a corner so his signs could be read from two directions. And Sally loved the upstairs. There was an area for a kitchen and a parlor, and two private bedrooms, one large and one a bit smaller. And of course, the bathroom was a big hit with everybody.

You didn't even have to pump the water, Katie noticed when it came time for her to walk through the building. There were taps that you just turned off and on!

The downstairs had plenty of room for a hardware—and a gunsmith's shop, Teddy said. The boy was figuring to take on two trades, it seemed, which was pretty much, if you asked Slocum. But he kept his mouth shut. Teddy was his own man now.

There was enough room up front for a counter and racks to store things like nails and screws and nuts and bolts, and to hang tools, like hammers and saws. Behind that was a place Teddy had already christened the "paint room," plus another area for wire samples and such. Out back, in the property's shed, was where he'd store the reels of wire and chicken fence and such, he told Slocum.

The rent on the place was only a hundred dollars a month, but Teddy had gone all out and bought the place outright. "First property I ever owned," he proudly confided to Slocum.

And then there was the wedding. Both Katie and Slocum stood up for them, and even though it was held in the judge's office, they had flowers and music, and it was real nice. Especially for the women. Both Sally and Katie cried through the whole thing. Slocum hoped the tears they shed were out of happiness.

They were. When the vows were over and it was time for Ted to kiss his bride, he did so passionately, with gusto and vigor. Katie later confided to Slocum that she'd never seen anything so beautiful as those two kids.

Slocum wasn't nearly so sappy as Katie, but he was proud enough to bust his buttons. He was as proud of Ted as if he were his own son, and just seeing him there, like a fully grown man taking grown-up vows and signing grown-up papers, brought tears to his eyes, too. He didn't exactly cry, but he did a lot of blinking.

And then there was the furniture shopping, which Slocum gladly refused. Furnishing a house and picking out linens and such just wasn't his idea of a good time. Besides, he thought they were rushing it. After all, the shop wouldn't be finished until next week, and they still had to order supplies. Hell, Slocum didn't even know where you got supplies for a hardware!

But Teddy did. He had already sent away for wholesale catalogs, and had already talked to a blacksmith, who agreed to fabricate some of the things he'd need.

It looked to Slocum like Teddy was pretty much set.

The one thing that bothered him, though, was that Teddy would still remember what he'd done, and have to pay for it. Marshal Pete was sure on his tail. Practically every corner he turned had a U.S. deputy marshal hanging around on the other side.

"You fellers patrol a lot?" Slocum asked the fourth or fifth one he practically collided with. He'd never before seen them out in such numbers.

"Just lately," the deputy confided, then spoke no more.

But Slocum knew. They were keeping tabs on Teddy round-the-clock. He decided to go visit Pete.

He walked straight into the U.S. marshal's office and asked for him, only to be told that he was out on patrol.

"Him, too?" Slocum asked the deputy on duty. "Jesus Christ!"

The young deputy, who looked wet behind the ears, and who Slocum hadn't seen before, appeared innocent of absolutely everything, and so Slocum stalked off, growling, "Tell Pete I'll be back. And tell him I said to lay off Teddy."

"Y-yessir," the deputy said, blinking. "What was your name?"

The deputy was practically shaking in his boots.

"Tell him Slocum was here," he said, and let the door slam behind him.

But Slocum didn't make it back that day. In fact, he didn't make it back until after dark.

At about six o'clock, Katie and the newlyweds hadn't returned to Katie's place, and so Slocum—who was constantly in Iris's sites—decided to eat out. He walked up the street, noticing the quiet and all the CLOSED signs. Phoenix was a nice town, but they rolled up the sidewalks awful early.

But then he neared the saloon, and that was a whole different story. Lights blared out into the street, and music and laughter as well. He took a hard left at the batwing doors. He hoped they had something to eat as well as drink, but if they didn't, he figured he could muddle through on beer.

He was in luck, however. A small sign hanging over the bar stated, RESTAURANT IN BACK, so he just followed the sign. He went through a door in the rear and walked into a dark, romantic little café. Whoever had decorated the saloon hadn't been allowed in the back, because there sure wasn't anything gaudy about it.

Slocum was wondering if *he* fit in, when a young lady— and he meant lady, nothing like the whores working the front room—came up and asked, "May I seat you, sir?"

"Sure thing," he said, and followed her to a small table. Before he had a chance to sit down, she asked, "Will anyone else be joining you?"

When he answered, "No," she sat him down and offered him a menu, then left him alone.

He saw that he wasn't alone in the place. Most of the other tables were filled with couples. And just when he was thinking that he sure wouldn't lead a good woman through that saloon, he saw another door at the back. Well, the back of the saloon, but the front was toward the next street. The building must go all the way through.

He ordered a big steak, along with a baked potato with sour cream and plenty of butter, creamed corn, and green salad, and while he was at it, a dessert of cherry cobbler with real ice cream!

While he sat back and waited, he lit a ready-made and looked around the room, studying faces. In a way, they were his stock-in-trade. But his eyes stopped on a man sitting three tables from him, a man dining alone, as was he, a man just finishing his meal.

The face was familiar, and it took him a few seconds to make the link; it was Rodney Morris, a feller wanted for murder in three states and territories.

Slowly, Slocum pushed back his chair and stood up. Slowly, he made his way over to Morris's table and moved between diners to stand behind the man's chair. His hand clasped Morris's shoulder.

Morris tried to whip around toward him, but his spurs got tangled in the chair's legs, and he ended up falling over. But not all the way. Slocum grabbed him under the arm and hauled him up—also relieving him of his gun—before the chair hit the floor without him.

"Rodney Morris?" Slocum said. "You're under arrest for murdering three people and whatever else you done that ain't caught up with you yet." Slocum slid Morris's gun into his belt, then headed toward the door.

"Go ahead and serve my supper," he said to the befuddled waiter. "I'm takin' him to jail."

Slocum marched Morris out the front door, around the sidewalk to the front of the saloon, then down toward the marshal's office.

"What kinda lawdog eats in a fancy restaurant?" Morris asked as they crossed an alley.

"The hungry kind, I guess," Slocum said. "Keep movin'!" he ordered when Morris tried to pause.

"I'm movin', I'm movin'!" came the reply. "Y'don't need to get so grumpy about it."

"Grumpy?" snorted Slocum. "Were you feelin' grumpy the night you killed little Cora Kingman over in El Paso? Were you feelin' grumpy when you killed that marshal in New Mexico or the storekeeper up in Colorado Springs?"

There was no reply.

"C'mon," said Slocum, poking Morris in the back with the barrel of his gun. "Move it."

"Why? So's you can take me down an alley and club me to death?"

Slocum snorted. "Don't go givin' me ideas."

They walked down the street, then crossed over to the other side, where there were lights on in the marshal's office. Somebody was home anyway.

Slocum pushed the door open, then shoved Morris inside. The young deputy was nowhere in sight, but there was another at a desk, doing paperwork. "Help you?" he said.

"I'm Slocum. Tell Pete I got another one for 'im. Rodney Morris, wanted for murder." He gave Morris another little shove, but this time he reacted all out of proportion, falling forward and landing on a table on his belly.

Quicker than snap, he was up again and whirling around, and butting Slocum in the belly with his head. Slocum was knocked back against the wall before the deputy could get up from behind his desk.

Slocum didn't think twice. The Colt was still in his hand, and he used it. Not to kill, but to wound. He hit him in the right shoulder, and he figured Morris wouldn't be hefting anything heavier than an ink pen for quite some time.

The bullet's hit spun Morris around, right into the deputy's clutches. And after the deputy got him on his feet, he said, "Hang on, Slocum," and took Morris back to the cell block.

He had no more disappeared through the cell block door than the outside door burst in. It was Pete, gun out, shouting, "What's goin' on in here?"

"You're too late," said Slocum, from the floor. "That party's over, I reckon."

"Jesus Christ," Pete muttered, holding down a hand to him and helping him up. "Tell me what happened."

"Only if you'll let me buy you a steak. You had any chuck yet?"

"Perfect timing, Slocum. I didn't have no lunch, and I could eat a raw buffalo right about now."

Slocum limped toward the door. "Well I can't promise you raw buffalo. Steak do instead?"

"Do me fine."

Just then, the door in back opened and the deputy walked in.

"There you are, Seth," Pete called. "Was beginning to figure you were doin' your paperwork in the outhouse."

"Real funny, Pete," replied Deputy Seth. He nodded toward Slocum and said, "He brung in a man. I was just puttin' him in a cell. He's a tricky bastard. You best watch 'im."

"Wanna tell me who he is?"

"Oh, sorry, Pete," the deputy said. "He's Rodney Morris, right Slocum?"

Slocum nodded, antsy to get back to the restaurant and his steak.

"Pete . . ." he said.

"All right, I'm comin'," Pete said. "Hold the fort, Seth!" He started toward the front door, then stopped cold. "Hey Slocum, you know you're limping?"

Slocum, whose left hip was hurting like a bastard, said, "It's temporary, dammit. C'mon! Don't want my steak to go gettin' cold!"

Epilogue

Later, while Pete cleaned his plate, Slocum sat back, enjoying a ready-made. The bad guys just seemed to be dropping into his lap lately, and he couldn't help wondering if it had something to do with Teddy. Teddy'd brought him luck, all right.

But everything eventually came to an end, and Slocum had the feeling that maybe this was it. Once he left Teddy behind, there wouldn't be any more easy catches, no more "fortunate" deaths. It would just be him again, just Slocum. And just Teddy—with Sally, of course.

He had mulled this over a hundred times, and what it boiled down to was that he'd be sad to leave Teddy. Teddy, despite their short acquaintance, had become like the son he never had. That he knew of anyway.

And tearing himself away at this stage, when everything seemed new and fresh and bright, when Teddy's future seemed to glisten before him, was almost more than he could bear.

It was an odd feeling for the big man, one he hadn't

much experience with. At this level anyhow. It was why, midafternoon, he had let the others go on furniture shopping without him. It wasn't just boring, it was painful!

He'd felt hot tears pushing at his eyes during the wedding ceremony. Not tears of sorrow or loss, but tears for himself, that he wouldn't be around the man-boy any longer, wouldn't be around to hold his first baby, wouldn't be there to see him experience a lot of firsts.

And then, it all clicked into place for him.

He wasn't feeling sorry for himself. Why? Because Slocum never felt sorry for himself, that was why!

He stubbed out his smoke on his empty plate. He'd had it with self-pity, was sick of mourning something that wasn't even dead. Why, he'd be back through Phoenix again, probably sooner than he wanted!

And Ted? Well, Ted would be fine. He had Sally to take care of now, and she was there to take care of him. They'd both be fine.

There was one thing niggling at the back of his skull, though. Katie. Well, he'd be back for her, sooner or later. When his feet stopped itching anyhow. He and Katie could grow old together, sitting lazily on their front porch, her with her knitting and him whittling. And they could have Ted and Sally over once a week for a meal.

He didn't know that Katie would take to anybody calling her "grandma," but at this point, he'd almost pay the kids to call him "gramps." It sounded nice. It sounded homey.

"Where you goin' next?" Pete asked, working his napkin between his hands.

Slocum shrugged. "I dunno. New Mexico, California, maybe Colorado. You tell me. Where're all the big-ticket bad boys hangin' out lately?"

DON'T MISS A YEAR OF

Slocum Giant
by
Jake Logan

Slocum Giant 2004:
Slocum in the Secret
Service

Slocum Giant 2005:
Slocum and the Larcenous
Lady

Slocum Giant 2006:
Slocum and the Hanging
Horse

Slocum Giant 2007:
Slocum and the Celestial
Bones

Slocum Giant 2008:
Slocum and the Town
Killers

Slocum Giant 2009:
Slocum's Great
Race

Slocum Giant 2010:
Slocum Along
Rotten Row